MW00805495

Love Thy Neighbor

A PRECARIOUS ENDEAVOR

By award-winning author,

LINDA BELLO-RUIZ

LOVE THY NEIGHBOR

A Precarious Endeavor

By award-winning author

Linda Bello-Ruiz

www.mariahpublishing.com

ISBN: 978-0-9895258-5-5
Published by Mariah Publishing, California
www.mariahpublishing.com
Cover design by Yoko Matsuoka
Typography by Yoko Matsuoka
Back cover author photograph by Ric Ewing
Interior design by Leo Craton
Content editing by Jan Arzooman
Printed in the United States of America

❧Dedications❧

Debra Jane Sargent Bouillerce

July 20, 1951-August 3, 2016

Thank you, Debi for allowing me the precious hours of our friendship during your final "rally" in late July, 2016. Thank you for digging deep for the strength to go with me for pedicures and manicures and shopping at Target to buy that new black purse you wanted.

The following day, you sat up in bed with popcorn, soda and candy bars in hand and graciously listened to me read the first twenty chapters of this manuscript. At the end, you clapped your hands and with tears encouraged me to finish the manuscript and get the story to the world.

I dedicate this book to you my dearest friend of over fifty years. I know you are now resting in peace. Yours was a brave fight and you didn't give up easily. I love you, Debi.

Marsha Lea Ewing-Hernandez

May 24, 1940 – September 4, 2016

To my dear sister, Marsha. You are gone now, but forever in my heart. Thank you for being a wonderful big sister. You loved this story and wanted to hear every new chapter on its completion.

"Mom and Dad would be very proud of you, Sis," you said, after I read you the first thirty chapters. Thank you. I will always hold your words near to my heart. You were a big part of my life, especially in Mexico. I love you, Sis.

May you and Debi find each other in Heaven. I have felt both of your spirits on a daily basis, encouraging me as I write...inspiring me to the end.

❧Wanderings❧

To look beyond what I cannot see
To watch a beautiful story unfold
To see through life's illusions
To witness a story that is yet untold

A wonderful place to wander through
Landscapes on an unending scroll
Words laying in spaces and cracks
Trying to reach the song of our soul

Seeds of hope planted therein
The sun of faith shinning inside
Treasures in places to be found
Weavings of God growing out of the ground

Joanne Kenzy
July 6, 2016

❧Acknowledgements❧

It takes a village to complete challenging tasks, and that's especially true when writing a book. Writing is a solitary task, so having a village of friends is priceless.

Thank you goes to the Faith Writers of Lincoln Hills—Jan, Jeri, Joanne, Dory, and Beth—for reading chapters and offering suggestions and edits along the way. Thank you, Stan Keach for reading each chapter in its first draft—bravely letting me know when scenes made sense and when they didn't. Jo Chandler, fellow-author and friend, thank you for reading chapters and giving me direction. To another fellow-author and friend of many years, Quentin Grady, your input was spot-on.

Jan Arzooman, your eye to detail and knowledge of conceptual-editing polished this story and I am grateful. A big hug and thanks goes to my friend, Mary Smith for listening. You patiently listened to me read the entire manuscript in its final form and offered valuable advice.

Leo Craton, I appreciate your friendship and your excellent book formatting skills. Thank you.

Gracias also goes to Nelly, Esteben, Veronica, and Daniel for your precious memories which I added to mine. In places where there was nobody to guide me, I used my imagination, making this a work of fiction, inspired by actual events.

This is a work of fiction inspired by actual events.

❧Preface❦

November, 2010

Stress settled around my shoulders like a heavy cloak. The bass from the stereo speakers next door pounded throughout the house, keeping time with my pulsating blood pressure.

As the sun began to set, I slumped into the black and red cushions of my rocking chair and stared out the open French doors of my bedroom. The tall palm trees in the front yard swayed in the evening breeze while two black ravens fluffed their feathers and drank water from the pool. Normally, this scene would be soothing, but tonight irritation consumed me.

My name is Rebecca and I'm from California, living several months a year in La Perlita, a small fishing village off the Pacific Coast of Mexico. I've been visiting this piece of paradise for over forty years. I purchased my land back in the eighties when there were few hotels and only a handful of ocean-view restaurants. Half the town faces the Pacific Ocean while the other half consists of acres of farmland and palm tree groves that lead down to a freshwater lagoon. At the time, my two adjoining corner lots were nothing more than tiny squares on a realtor's map in the midst of those groves.

After ten years of construction, I now live in a beautiful home of custom brick arches and massive pillars. I've landscaped the front yard with a lawn, palms, bright-red bougainvillea, and an inviting blue-tiled pool, all hidden behind ten-foot walls.

But havoc has pierced my paradise.

Toro Rivera, the area drug trafficker, and his young family have moved into the brick-and-mortar house next to me, and they've opened a small-scale beer store right on our adjoining corner wall. The screeching of the rolling, metal security door opening and shutting, the clanging of bottles, loud music, and motorcycles shatter my once-serene environment.

"Lord, make the noise go away," I plead each night as their partying continues on into the sunrise hours.

I have complained to anyone who will listen as well as the mayor and county administrator. The response has been the same. "There's nothing you can do, except move. Toro Rivera is too influential and has the police in his back pocket."

Moving is not an option. This is my refuge and I refuse to leave. Toro and his family have to go.

My frustration has increased as weeks pass without resolution by the authorities. The beer store never closes. At times, I look outside the upstairs living room window to the sidewalk below to see men relieving themselves against my privacy wall, too drunk or lazy to walk a block away and do their business amongst the coconut palms.

Now the neighbor has thirty-five goats corralled behind his house. Goats have their place in this village, but not next to my house. The smell of dung and urine waft through the upstairs windows.

Toro Rivera is not somebody I want to mess with on my own. I glance in his direction when I walk by his house on the way to the store. His massive frame and round, hard-lined face encourages me to hurry by.

The rocking chair in my bedroom keeps pace with my pulsating emotions. My resentment turns to anger. From the open Bible resting on my lap, Matthew 22:39 stares up at me. "Love thy neighbor."

"Are you kidding me, Lord?" I blurt, looking upward. "Love my neighbor? This has to be a joke."

Does God or anyone else expect me to love a drug-dealing neighbor—an unrighteous, law-breaking young man? Maybe it was just a coincidence that the Bible laid open to that verse.

I drifted back to a time in my late teens when I'd lived with a low-level drug dealer and used drugs—mostly marijuana. But that was a long time ago and I am no longer that young girl.

I've felt led to take risks at other times in my life. Not long after leaving my abusive, drug-dealing boyfriend, I left the comforts of my home in the United States to live in Costa Rica and to open a half-way house. I spent nights in the Red Light Zone of San Jose, talking to young prostitutes and street girls, inviting them to leave the streets and start a new life under my care.

Had those life experiences been a prelude to what I now feel led to do?

I closed the good book on my lap and closed my eyes. The tension and anger began to lift.

Who was I to question God? He'd given me guidance and strength so many times before in my life.

So, that same day, I set out to love my neighbor, Toro Rivera.

This is our story.

PART ONE ~ TORO
1996 – 2010

𝕯CHAPTER ONE𝕾

Fourteen years earlier, 1996

The eleven-year-old boy gripped the old slingshot, jumped over the pile of broken bricks, steadied his aim, and fired. A small pebble hit the moss-colored iguana in the head, knocking it out of the palm tree.

"*Hecho*! Done!" Toro shouted to two of his younger brothers who scampered up behind him. "We'll have iguana soup for dinner."

Wrapping his big-brother arms around Esteben and Julio, he pushed them forward. "Take the kill to *Mamá*." He picked up the net at his feet. "I'm going to the lagoon to see what I can catch."

The oldest of five, Toro envied his brothers' freedom. Once their classes ended at midday, they roamed free in the small fishing village of La Perlita off the southern Pacific Coast of Mexico. They jumped into whatever adventures their wild hearts could find. But Toro now carried the burden of helping his father support the family.

A few weeks earlier, his heart had tumbled to the pit of his stomach hearing his father's words change his future. "School is a luxury we don't have, Son. It's time you leave school and go to work with me, fishing."

"But Papá, I'm only in fifth grade. I don't want to leave school." Toro knew that other kids in the Barrio quit school to work, but he wanted to finish elementary and even middle school. "I want to be a Chivas defender like Claudio Suárez. Not a fisherman."

"Stop dreaming, Toro. People like us don't become famous soccer players."

Toro hung his head. He treasured his Suárez jersey, a rare Christmas gift from an uncle. He never missed a Chivas game, which he watched on their old black-and-white television. *I don't want to be a fisherman.*

"My father took me out of school in third grade to work in the fields. Consider yourself lucky," his father said. "It's time to face reality."

Toro looked to his mother, Maria, for support. He glimpsed anger in her eyes as she stared at his father. Then her face became expressionless—as if she'd disappeared, again, into herself. He didn't understand grownup things, but he knew that ever since his father started drinking heavily a few years earlier, his mother acted afraid. He knew from experience she would not go against his father's strong will.

Toro watched his mother slump her shoulders and walk silently out of the room, taking his hope for a reprieve with her.

～

The next morning, as his four younger brothers slept—most likely dreaming of sling shots and iguanas—Toro arose before dawn, ate a tortilla stuffed with eggs and salsa, and shuffled out the door behind his father. After their silent fifteen-minute walk to the docks at the lagoon, Enrique powered up the motor of his yellow *panga* and guided the motorboat around the point that separated the expansive fresh water lagoon from the salty Pacific Ocean.

"Let's pray to the sea gods to catch enough fish to sell at the fish market today, Son," Enrique shouted into the wind. "We need to pay the rent and put food on the table."

Toro set the fishing poles, lures, nets, spears, and a bag of bait on the floor of the boat and plopped himself onto the forward seat, his small frame leaving plenty of room on both sides.

"I hate being poor," he muttered, wiping the saltwater spray off his face. He envied those kids in town with nice clothes, new bikes, sober fathers—kids waking up for school today. He wanted to scream. Instead, he crossed his arms across his chest and scowled in frustration.

"Why are you sulking?" his father, Enrique, yelled a few seconds later. "You got a problem?"

Toro shook his head, afraid to open his mouth. He missed the joy of walking to school with his brothers, giving his teachers a hard time, joking around with his classmates, and playing soccer at recess. But, he dared not cross his father. Over the past few years, he'd felt that heavy hand alongside his head too many times. He knew to duck and run, or swallow his anger and resentment.

"Keep an eye out for other fishermen bringing in a catch," Enrique yelled over the roar of the motor.

3

Toro nodded. Thirty minutes later he called out, "Over on the right," and motioned to two boats up ahead. "They're heading toward the flock of seagulls by those rocks!"

His father changed course. "That means a school of forage fish. Let's hope for marlin, dorado, or tuna."

The squawking and chirping of the seagulls increased as they approached. Enrique slowed the panga and Toro set out the poles and lures as his father instructed. They began circling the large rock formation, waiting.

Moments later, under the distant caws of seagulls gathering, the pole closest to Toro suddenly bowed.

"You've got something there, Son. Start reeling it in," Enrique bellowed, shutting off the motor.

Toro reeled and reeled. The fish fought to get away. "Faster!" his father demanded.

"I am!" Toro screamed back, his muscles shaking.

"Give it to me." Enrique grabbed the pole and pushed Toro aside.

Toro sulked as his father fought the large fish for nearly a half hour.

Muscles straining under his dirty t-shirt, Enrique brought the fish to the side of the boat. "It's a blue marlin. Here. Hold the pole steady. I'll get the hook."

Toro held onto the pole for dear life. *Hurry. If I lose this fish, he'll never forgive me.*

Within moments, his father hooked the side of the marlin and Toro helped bring it on board. "It's huge," Toro said, collapsing onto the seat, wiping perspiration from his brow.

"At least a hundred pounds," his father replied, with a big smile on his face. "This is what I'm talking about, Son. With catches like this, we can support the family."

He secured the marlin on the floor of the boat, slammed a short bat into its forehead killing it instantly, and smacked his son on the back. "Good job. Let's catch a few more."

In spite of his resentment, Toro couldn't help feeling pride about the catch. He gave his father a nervous smile. "I still want to be a soccer player though," he thought.

Toro motored out with his father Monday through Saturday. Sometimes the family had enough food on the table and other times they ate rice, beans, tortillas, and the occasional iguana. They paid rent and electricity when able, and on occasion they feared eviction from their dilapidated, two-bedroom brick house.

Esteben, Toro's nine-year-old brother, offered to help. "I'll leave school and get a job, too," he told Toro one night as they lay in their crowded bedroom. The soft breathing of Miguel and Ricky, along with the crickets singing outside the window, could not drown out their parents fighting in the room across the hall.

"Me, too. I'll help," chimed in seven-year-old Julio.

Toro took a deep breath in the darkness and closed his dark-brown eyes. *I'm the oldest. My brothers need me to look out for them. Papá won't. Mamá can't. I want them to be more than poor fishermen.* "No. You will both stay in school," he said. "Now go to sleep."

❧

An hour later, Toro lay on the top bunk still staring at the old ceiling paint. With clenched teeth and hands curled into fists, he listened to his mother's sobs—hating himself for not being brave enough to protect her from his father fists.

We used to be happy. We spent holidays with Mamá's family in Michoacán. Papá played soccer with us after Sunday Mass. Now he's angry or drunk. I can't explain where things went wrong.

❧

Over the next two years, Toro accompanied his father in the panga, learning the trade. He willed himself to forget his childhood dream of becoming a professional soccer player—and watched that dream fly away like seagulls over the horizon.

"We need more fish. More money!" his father shouted as he stumbled, drunk, out of the boat after a particularly dismal fishing day.

Embarrassed, Toro watched him stagger on the dock. "Papá, let me help or you'll fall in the lagoon."

"Get away from me. I don't need help!"

"There's got to be a way," Toro thought, gathering fishing gear and tossing a bag of empty beer cans into a nearby trash can. *This can't be my life.* He noticed two older boys in the slip next to him, readying their pangas to guide tourists around the bay. "That's it," he said to nobody in particular and started his walk home that hot afternoon.

❧

The next day, after fishing with his father in the morning, Toro cleaned the stench of fish out of the boat with chlorine, changed his clothes, and passed a comb through his thick black hair. When ready, he stood on the docks with his engaging smile. "Excursions!" he shouted, as tourists walked by. "Take a trip out into the lagoon to see the egrets, turtles, and crocodiles. Just twenty dollars."

A group of girls in shorts, bikini tops and sunglasses passed by and smiled.

Toro could tell they were tourists by their blond hair and skimpy clothes. He turned on his thirteen-year-old charm. "Come, beautiful *chicas*. I take you for a ride."

The group chatted among themselves for a moment. He heard one of them say, "Isn't he adorable?"

Toro kept the smile on his cherub face and crossed his fingers behind his back.

"Okay," the oldest woman in the group said, plopping a wide-brimmed hat on her head.

Toro held out his hand to guide them into the boat. "Welcome. You will enjoy this ride, *señoritas*."

Within a week, Toro pocketed an extra sixty dollars. When he had enough gas in the boat, he'd yell, "Only fifty dollars to spend four hours out to sea. Don't miss seeing whales, dolphins, and hidden beaches."

❧

Two weeks later, Toro drummed his fingers on the kitchen table. "Mamá, we're going to be late if Papá doesn't get up soon," he said. "The best fishing is before sunrise."

"Go try to wake him again, Toro," his mother encouraged.

Frustration showed in his eyes, but he obeyed. Standing by the bed in his parent's room, Toro nudged his father. "Papá. Wake up. We have to get going. The sun will be up soon."

"Damn it, Toro. Leave me alone!" his father slurred.

"Papá!"

"Go without me. You're thirteen now. You know how to fish."

Furious, Toro walked out of the house with resentment choking him. *We'll always be poor. He spends more on drinking tequila and beer with his amigos than we can bring in...no matter how much extra work I do.*

Several times a week, Enrique found reasons to stay home in bed. Each time, Toro filled in the gap and worked harder to keep food on the table.

Enrique stumbled into the kitchen one Sunday in April. "I'm going back to Michoacán, to the family ranch," he announced. "I can work with my brothers making more money than I'm making here."

Toro stopped eating and stared. His mother, Maria, sat in silence, touching a fresh bruise on her cheek.

Toro gave voice to his fear. "You're leaving—or we're all leaving?"

"I'm going first. I'll be back in a few weeks. Toro, you're in charge."

Toro smiled into his cereal bowl.

∽

"*Mamá*, here's a thousand pesos," Toro said with pride a week after his father's departure. "That's five boat rides and a good catch this morning. This will pay the rent and utilities. I'll have more next week."

"Thank you," Maria said, hugging Toro. "You're a good son. I'm proud of you. Why don't you take some of your earnings and buy yourself something? You deserve it."

"I will when we have enough food on the table and my brothers have enough to stay in school," he replied, feeling all grownup.

∽

Life in the Rivera home changed. Toro felt the anger, fear and tension disappear with his father's absence. His mother listened to foot-stomping *ranchera* music on the old radio during the day and her friends stopped by in the evenings to sit outside and crochet while their children played together in the street.

"I'm going into the town market," Maria told her sons on a Saturday morning. "Play near the house until Toro returns from fishing. Esteben, keep your eye on Ricky."

"All right, Mamá. What are you buying at the market?" he asked, buckling his younger brother's tattered sandals.

"I'm not buying today," his mother answered, with a big smile on her face. "I've crocheted three dozen doilies and I'm hoping to sell them to the tourists. Your godmother, Beatriz, will share the costs of a table with me at the market."

Eleven-year-old Esteben matched his mother's smile, happy to see the excitement in her face.

⊷

Then, two months after his hasty departure, Enrique's large frame once again filled the doorway.

"Papá!" screamed four-year-old Ricky, the youngest of the family, as he ran to hug his father's legs. "You're back!"

Enrique ruffled Ricky's black curly hair.

The other brothers, Esteben, Julio, and Miguel, followed Ricky while Toro sat at the kitchen table wondering what his father's return meant.

"We're going back to Santana," Enrique said. He gave his wife a quick hug. "But right now, I need a drink. I'll be back." With that, he abruptly left for the short walk to the corner store.

Maria stared after her husband. They had moved from Santana to La Perlita when Toro was three and Esteben one. She knew there had been a falling out between her husband and his father—a battle that had raged unresolved for over ten years. Although Enrique refused to explain, she believed the stubborn anger between father and son had caused her husband's excessive drinking. *And now he wants to return?*

"I don't want to leave La Perlita and move to Michoacán. This is my home. My village!" Toro blurted out. "He can go and just leave us alone."

"We're a family. Where your father goes we must follow, my son. Obviously, your father decided he can't support us here any longer. Fishing barely keeps a roof over our heads and food on our table—let alone covering the costs of keeping your brothers in school."

Toro dropped his spoon, unable to finish his breakfast. "Mama, I've been able to pay our bills for the last two months. I'll get a second job. Construction. That will help," he insisted.

"Mamá, I'll leave school and help Toro fish. And we can sell vegetables, too," Esteben offered.

Maria wrapped her arms around Esteben's small frame. "No, *mis hijos*. Your papá has made the decision. We knew he was coming back for us. We'll go to the family ranch and be farmers like your grandparents and uncles. It is best."

"No! I won't go!" Toro shouted. His round, brown face felt hot with rage.

Hearing Toro's outburst from outside, Enrique stepped into the small living room like an angry bear. "Do NOT disrespect your mother!" He slapped his eldest son across the face with the back of his calloused hand.

The younger children hid behind their mother.

Toro stared at his father, hate coursing through his veins.

Oblivious to anyone's feelings, Enrique collapsed into the rustic wooden chair at the nearby kitchen table. "We leave on the Sunday bus. I'll sell the panga for the bus fare. You have three days to pack your things and say goodbye to your friends," he snapped.

He finished his bottle of beer and opened a new one.

"Maria! Where's my food?"

Toro stormed out of the house, ran through the palm trees and past the banana grove until, out of breath, he reached the lagoon—

his quiet retreat. Sweat poured from his brow, beading its way in silent ripples onto his temple, into his dark angry eyes.

"No!" he shouted to a crocodile lazing in the late afternoon sun. "I won't go." He clenched his fists. "I don't need them. I'll just make it on my own."

The large reptile slipped back into the water and half a dozen white egrets took flight from the slippery bank.

⌀

Hours later, his anger in check, Toro walked the ten minutes back home, kicking rocks and dirt with his old brown huaraches. Pebbles lodged in the broken soles of his sandals, which flip-flopped like the jaws of a hungry crocodile.

Tears formed, and he wiped them away with the back of his hands. He loved living in La Perlita. Alone, and with his brothers Esteben and Julio, Toro had explored the area for miles. He knew every palm and banana tree between his home and the lagoon in one direction, and his home and the Pacific Ocean in the other.

I'm not leaving!

He had three days to take charge of his future.

◌CHAPTER TWO◌

Toro rose early the following morning and headed straight to the home of Joaquin Hernandez—the best-known and most-respected builder in the small village.

The previous evening, he begged his father to let him stay in La Perlita. "Papá, please," he said. "I'll take care of myself. I'll work hard."

"What do you think you can do, Toro?" his father said with scorn.

"Construction. I'll work in construction. Please. I don't want to leave."

"You're too scrawny to work construction, Son. You're coming with us to Santana."

"Please, Papá. You'll have one less mouth to feed. I promise to send you money."

His father finally agreed and Toro now hoped he wouldn't change his mind in the sober light of day.

"Don Joaquin," he stammered, when the tall, muscular man opened the door. He was wearing Levis and a long-sleeved shirt. "So sorry to bother you. I'm looking for work."

"Whose son are you?" the man asked, stepping into the air, closing the house door behind himself.

Toro spoke quickly, fearing he'd lose his nerve. "Son of Enrique Rivera and Maria Ramos. I need work. My family is leaving for Santana, Michoacán, on Sunday. I am not going with them."

"How old are you?"

"Almost fourteen," Toro said, standing up straight.

"What's your construction experience, young man?"

"None, sir. But I am strong and learn fast. I've been fishing and driving tourists in our panga. But my father is selling it. I will work as a laborer for you, mixing mortar, carrying bricks, digging holes—anything."

"And where will you live?" the gruff-looking man asked.

"In the Barrio where we have lived for years—for as long as I can remember."

"Your father is Enrique, the fisherman, yes? Let me speak to him this afternoon and see what he says."

"*Gracias, Señor Hernandez.* You will see I am a good worker, and he will say yes. I'll come see you Monday morning." His confident reply masked the nervousness in the pit of his stomach.

La Perlita is my home, he reminded himself on the way back home.

This is where he learned to fish on the open sea with both line and net. During coconut season, he raced his friends up the palm trees and with a short, thick stick knocked the ripe fruit to the ground for his brothers to gather. He felt pride that he made extra money for his family driving tourists around the lagoon in the panga. He could not move inland, away from all he knew and cherished.

∽

Saturday night, with his near-future decided, Toro sat on his lumpy straw mattress and leaned against the rough concrete wall. His four brothers sat on their bunk beds listening as Toro informed them he wouldn't be going to Santana with them. Their downcast faces spoke of their sadness, but only little Ricky shed tears.

Toro saw Esteben fighting to hold back his emotions. "Toro, what will we do without you? Who will we run to when Papá starts to yell and hit?"

"You'll all be okay. Esteben, you take care of your brothers now. Keep them away from Papá when he's angry or drunk. Just keep running and ducking like we've been doing for years."

"But Toro, he'll just move us up there and then take us out of school to work in the fields," Julio said, concern on his face. "I don't want to leave school."

Toro kept his voice steady. "He may try to do that. He said he wouldn't. I've promised to send money so all of you can at least get from primary into middle school—maybe even complete high school. I can't let him take away your dreams, too."

❧CHAPTER THREE❧

On Monday morning, Toro awoke to an empty house. He didn't have a clock, but the sun was rising. Panicked, he threw on a pair of jeans and an old t-shirt, and stepped outside into the early, muggy June morning.

Don Joaquin had told Toro he'd drive him to the construction site. As he walked to his new boss's house, he felt alone for the first time in his almost fourteen years. His mother's and brother's goodbye tears the day before clung to him, along with the memory of his father's stern, unyielding face.

Why didn't I just swallow the anger and follow my family to Santana?

Too late now.

Toro hurried down the dirt road into town. Despite the old pair of sneakers he wore, he walked with a confident swagger, shoulders back and head held high in an attempt to hide his loneliness. To the banana trees and the small lizards scurrying out of his path he said, "I can do this. I'm a man now. I don't need nobody."

"*Buenos dias, joven,*" Don Joaquin said as Toro arrived. He was standing near the red golf cart he used to get from one construction site to another.

"Good morning, Don Joaquin," Toro answered. He climbed into the cart, feeling dwarfed by Don Joaquin's big frame.

"You're five minutes late this morning. Don't let that happen again," Don Joaquin said gruffly.

"Sorry. I won't sir."

Don Joaquin nodded. "Are you ready for a full day's work in the heat, young man?"

"Yes, sir. I am used to working in the sun."

"That's good."

A few minutes later, Toro looked around at the construction site, not surprised that he recognized most of the other workers. He knew that fishing, boating, selling vegetables, and construction work were the fate of the able but uneducated segment of La Perlita.

Don Joaquin motioned for him to follow. "I'll start you mixing mortar. Use ten shovels full of sand to every bag of cement and add half of this small bag of lime. *Entiende*? Then add water. Don't add too much water to the mix or the bricks won't adhere. You got that?"

Toro nodded and got to work lifting fifty-pound bags of cement—almost falling under the weight. He lifted and emptied bag after bag and then added in the sand, lime and water. His muscles screamed for relief, but he refused to show any weakness.

At precisely two o'clock, eight tired but jovial workers collapsed under the nearby palm tree. Toro watched them take out the lunches their wives or mothers had delivered a few minutes earlier. He smelled the array of aromas—hot beans and garlic, savory meats, rice, and warm tortillas. His empty stomach grumbled. Unprepared to pack himself a lunch that first morning, he only had a left-over bread roll and two bananas, which he'd picked off a tree on the way to work.

"Hey, you, skinny-boy," Pablo, one of the older workers, called from across the way. "You worked hard this morning. Come here. Have some warm tortillas and *pollo*."

Toro nodded, not wanting to show his excitement. He moved to sit on the dirt next to Pablo and accepted the chicken taco with an embarrassed, "Thank you." The taco disappeared in one bite.

Pablo's large gut shook like jello as he laughed. "Slow down, *joven*, or you'll choke." He wrapped a second piece of chicken in a tortilla, added a few chili peppers, and handed it to Toro. "You're Enrique's son, right? We heard he went back to Michoacán. You're one brave youngster to stay here on your own. How about I have my wife pack a little extra food this week? Until you get your first pay. How's that sound?"

Toro smiled. "Yes. Thank you, Don Pablo. I would like that."

After lunch, Toro finished mixing the needed mortar and looked around for more to do.

"Take those bricks to the stone masons," Don Joaquin shouted from across the construction site, pointing to a large pile nearby.

Toro filled and pushed heavy wheelbarrows full of bricks to the workers, who stacked them one-by-one to build the walls of the house under construction. Afraid to complain and lose his job, he worked under the unrelenting sun nine hours per day, his undeveloped muscles cramping and burning.

At the end of the five-and-a-half-day work week, young Toro received his pay of 550 pesos, the equivalent of $55.00. And that first Saturday, and every Saturday afternoon thereafter, he stopped at the post office in town to send half of his pay to his family.

At the end of the first month, Toro realized he didn't have enough money to pay his rent. "Don Pablo," he asked during a lunch break, "do you know where I can live, cheap?"

Don Pablo contemplated for a few minutes. "How about you come live with my wife and me," he finally said. "We have a small room with a bed. It's not much, but you'll have a place to sleep. It'll cost you ten dollars a month, including your meals."

"Thank you, Don Pablo. That is very kind. Thank you."

Determined to be independent, Toro accepted his new life—work, sleep and sending money home for his brothers.

❧CHAPTER FOUR❧

Two years later, at sixteen, Toro looked like a man. He was sun-browned and handsome, standing six feet tall and weighing 180 pounds. Bulging biceps popped out from under his short-sleeved t-shirt—the payoff for those two years of manual labor.

Sitting on the curb outside the corner store one afternoon with a co-worker, a frustrated Toro tapped his fingers on his beer can. "I can't keep doing this. I'm making $70.00 a week now, but it's not enough to survive and send money to my family." He finished his cold Corona and crushed the can in his hand. "Damn. How will I ever get ahead?"

Alfonso, tall and lean, inhaled the last of his cigarette and flipped the butt to the ground at his feet. "There is another way," he said, staring off across the street.

Toro noticed him smiling at a group of young girls on their way home from middle school, clutching schoolbooks to their chests. He took in their white blouses and short blue skirts.

"There's a new guy strutting around town. Luis Camacho. He can't be that much older than us. He's bragging about how he's able to pocket thousands of pesos per week without breaking a sweat," Alfonzo said, lighting another cigarette.

"How?"

Alfonso looked around for a moment. "Nobody talks about it, but I found out he sells drugs—mostly marijuana. He lives in Autlan and has connections in Michoacán. He's looking for someone here to go into business with him."

Toro stared at the ground as Alfonso kept talking. "If you're interested, I'll ride up there with you to talk to him. It might be worth the two hour trip."

"Nah man. Too dangerous." Disdain showed in his eyes. "Once you're in that life, you don't get out...except in a box. I've heard the stories. That's not what I want." Toro hesitated. "I tried to become a police officer," he finally said.

"You what? Seriously?"

"I went into San Sebastian a couple of weeks ago. They're hiring. I filled out the paperwork."

"Why do you want to be police officer?"

Toro smiled. "I'm not afraid to confront *pendejo* idiots causing havoc. I like to solve problems. The pay is better than I get now. I don't have to work out in the hot sun. And...I can carry guns."

"All that fits you, man. So...when do you start?"

"I don't. They turned me down."

"Why?"

"Because I didn't finish grade school."

"I'm sorry, Toro. That sucks."

∽

In October of 2001, Toro made the eight-hour trip east into the hills of Michoacán, outside the rural town of Santana, to visit his family. He felt proud that at only sixteen he had provided the means for his brothers to remain in school. Esteben and Julio attended middle school in the mornings and worked alongside their father and uncle in the agricultural fields in the afternoons. His two younger brothers earned good grades in elementary school.

❧

"There's been changes here in the *campo*," his father told Toro during the visit.

"I can tell," he said, looking around the large backyard of his grandparent's home where his parents and brothers now lived. "Why did Grandpa and Grandma move?"

"They went to live in Morelia with your uncle Leo several months ago. But that's not what I'm referring to, Toro."

"What then, Papá?" he asked, confused.

Enrique lazed in a green and yellow hammock strung between two tall mango trees. Father and son drank tequila shots with beer chasers. Toro noticed deep lines in his dad's brow—lines that weren't there on his visit six months earlier.

"The farmers are growing marijuana in among the other crops," his father said, and then hesitated. "I am, too. We'll get good money for our efforts."

The dire implications of his father's words sent chills through Toro. Alarmed, he stood up. "Papá, why are you doing this?"

Too tall and strong now to fear his father's heavy hand, Toro nevertheless lowered his voice out of respect. "Once in, you're always in. Isn't that what you've always warned me about?"

"Yes, Son, but it's no longer a choice." His father practically spat the words.

"What do you mean?" Anger laced with fear filled his chest. He measured his words. "What have you gotten yourself and this family into?"

"We either grow *mota* for the cartel, or they'll take our land from us...and kill us!"

"Marijuana? Cartel? Take the land? Kill you? Have you talked to the police? Can't they help?"

"Growing up in La Perlita has made you very naïve, Son. Your grandfather and your uncles have resisted associating with organized crime for more than ten years. Instead, they supported the efforts of *La Familia* organization, citizens who vowed to rid this state of cartels and drugs."

Toro remained silent and watched his father toss back another shot of tequila.

"I didn't trust La Familia to protect anybody, Son," his father said with scorn. "They were a small group of vigilantes without power. When I saw the Valencia brothers and other drug cartels infiltrating the entire state of Michoacán, I knew we were in trouble. I begged your grandfather to sell the farm and leave. You were three and Esteben just a baby. I feared for your safety."

His father hesitated for a moment and Toro waited, having never heard this story before.

24

"My brothers and my father stood against me. We fought for weeks. Finally, against their wishes, I packed up and moved us to the Pacific Coast. Your grandfather called me a worthless coward. We didn't speak for years."

Toro mulled over the information, trying to put the pieces in perspective. "I'm confused. If you were so worried, and at war with your father, why did you come back?"

"My father is sick. Too old to work the land. My brother, Juan needed my help and assured me La Familia had a handle on this area." He took a deep breath. "I wanted to help my family and thought I could make more money here, selling vegetables and fruit, than fishing in La Perlita."

Toro paced around the backyard. "And now...what?"

Enrique pulled himself up out of the hammock and staggered. Impatient, Toro caught him and guided him to a chair. "What changed, Papá?"

Toro watched his father trying to compose himself. *He's drunk again!*

"A new government. A new president," Enrique slurred. "After seventy years, the Revolutionary Party and their dictatorship are gone."

"I know PRI lost the last election, but isn't that a good thing?" Toro asked, confused.

Enrique didn't respond.

Toro watched his father's chin collide with his chest and his arms fall limp to his sides. *Damn, he passed out.*

⊸⌇

Hours later, after the family finished dinner and his father slept off his binge, Toro played soccer with his brothers, basking in their laughter.

"We've missed you," Esteben said, punching his big brother in the shoulder.

"You think you can punch me?" Toro said, grabbing his fourteen-year-old brother around the chest and rubbing his knuckles into the top of his head. *He's still so small. He can't weigh more than a hundred pounds.*

Laughing, Esteben struggled to break free. "Help!" he yelled.

Julio jumped onto Toro's back and Miguel attacked him at the knees. The four boys tumbled onto the grass, wrestling and laughing.

"How'd you get so strong?" Esteben asked moments later as they lay on the grass looking at the night sky. "You working out?"

"Construction work is better than a gym, little Bro," he said, flexing his muscles like a weight lifter. "And why aren't you growing? Are you eating?"

"Yes. And I *am* growing. I'm almost five feet tall now. But, Mamá is worried. She says I was born tiny and I'll probably always be small. The doctors say I haven't hit my 'growth spurt' yet. I agree with the doctors...so just you wait, big brother. I'm coming for you!"

"You think I'm afraid?" Toro asked as he rolled over and pinned a laughing Esteben to the ground.

The following morning, Toro resumed the conversation with his father. "Papá, last night you said the PRI dictatorship had ended. *Why* isn't that a good thing?"

Enrique finished his coffee and placed his head in his hand. "Because as bad and corrupt as they were, they had the damn drug cartels under control."

Toro watched his father's brow begin to furrow, as if trying to find the right words.

"With this new government, it's like someone came in and started stomping on well-organized ant colonies. The *Federales* are killing off the top ants but the worker ants are running around like crazy, forming new colonies. There are so many cartels now, it's hard to keep them straight, Son."

"Which cartel is threatening you?" Toro asked, concerned.

"The Valencia brothers. They're a major cartel now. They're huge. Well-organized. Deadly. And, they're in alliance with the Colombians. They grow and traffic their own pot, along with poppies for heroin."

Enrique stopped a moment. "Maria! Bring me aspirin," he ordered.

Maria hurried into the kitchen, took aspirin out of the cupboard, and handed her husband a bottle of water from the refrigerator. Smiling at her son, she departed.

I wish he wouldn't order her around like that.

"The representative from the Valencias just levied a stiff tax against every business and landowner," his father continued. "He then pays kickbacks to the local police for protection. We can do nothing."

Alarmed, Toro leaned forward in his chair. "What is the La Familia organization doing about all of this? You just said they vowed to protect Michoacán. Are they?"

"Not entirely, but it is their plan, Toro."

His father's words startled him. Like most Mexicans, he listened to the news on television and read newspapers. But he hadn't realized that drugs and cartel activities were affecting his own family.

At that moment, Toro's uncle, Juan, stepped into the kitchen and maneuvered his girth into a plastic chair. The plastic groaned under his weight. "I see your father is telling you what's happening. By growing for the cartel, we'll be able to keep a portion of the marijuana crops and sell to a buyer down by Los Reyes," Juan said eagerly. "We won't be rich, but we won't be poor farmers any longer."

A chill lanced through Toro. "Tio Juan, how can you talk about this like it's nothing? How do you know how to grow *mota*? This family has grown sugar cane, vegetables, and berries for years— not drugs! How will you hide from the *Federales*? I saw military helicopters flying overhead just yesterday."

"It's easy. Our land is fertile. You plant the seedlings and leave them out in the sun and rain. The earth does the work. In just a few months, we'll have big plants shooting up to four feet."

"We're planting between other crops, in between giant rocks and even in the forest," Enrique added, pouring coffee for his brother.

How can this be happening? Shocked, Toro looked from his uncle to his father. "How long have you been doing this?"

"Just a few months—right after the Valencia cartel sent their men with assault rifles to persuade us to start planting. We have to do this, Son. Maria! Bring me a beer."

"Papá. Stop. Why do you order her around like that? The refrigerator is right behind you."

"Maria. Now!"

Toro stood and opened the refrigerator door. "Here," he said, handing his father a Corona. "Uncle, do you want a beer?"

"No, Sobrino. Gracias."

Settling back down at the table, Toro said. "You don't have to do what the cartel says, Papá. Leave here. Move back to La Perlita. We won't have luxuries, but we'll have freedom. You can go back to fishing. Esteben and Julio can help, or I'll get them a job in construction."

"No, Son," his father replied without emotion. "We can't."

"Don't say that, Papá. Get out now!"

"You don't get it, Toro. We have an agreement," his father said, looking at his brother, Juan. "We'll be okay. You go back to La Perlita."

"What about my brothers?"

Enrique stood to leave. "Esteben and Julio are working in the sugarcane and blackberry portions of the ranch. They'll be fine."

∽

After dinner that night, Toro kicked the soccer ball around the backyard with his brothers, enjoying their carefree energy and laughter. Six-year-old Ricky attempted to kick the ball between his big brother's legs, only to find himself lifted high into the air.

Toro laughed at Ricky's squeals of delight. He cherished these moments with his brothers.

A bit later, Toro visited with his mother in the kitchen as she washed the dishes. "*Mamá*, can't you make *Papá* leave and return to La Perlita? I hear stories. The cartels are evil. They torture and kill to enforce obedience. All they care about is the drug money and power. Please, if they've set up headquarters near here, it's not safe. They even kidnap and force young boys into their gang. Please, Mamá."

"Toro, I pray every day for our safety. I've begged your father to leave, as I heard you doing this afternoon. He won't listen. He's tired of being a poor peasant. There's money coming in now and there will be more with the January harvest. We'll be okay as long as we pay the Valencia cartel. It was your father and your uncle, Juan's idea to move your grandparents away, just in case. And please, don't send your hard-earned pesos anymore. I'll make sure the boys stay in school—and maybe even get them into high school if they want."

ക

On a November afternoon, a frustrated Toro caught the four o'clock bus out of Santana and headed back to his beloved seashore. Staring out the bus window, he watched acres and acres of lush, fertile fields roll by—valleys and hillsides covered with row after row of sugarcane, strawberries, and blackberries. Green plants and bushes bursting with a variety of vegetables extended up into tree lines to the mountaintop.

He now knew this beautiful part of the world was a drug growing paradise, run by the Valencia Cartel.

Feeling disgusted, angry, and powerless, Toro closed his eyes and silently prayed for the safety of his family, who refused to leave their thirty acres—land that had been in the Rivera family for over seventy years.

❧CHAPTER FIVE❦

The sunsets of La Perlita throw hues of orange, yellow, and pink into the sky, which intermingle with the cloud formations to create a breathtaking panorama of shifting beauty. That evening, just a few days after returning from Santana, Toro saw none of this magic as he sat on the pier. His mind ebbed and flowed like the waves below as he searched for ideas on how to protect his family.

Papá is putting my mom and my brothers at risk because of his own drunken desire for money. I don't know how, right this minute, but I swear I'll get my brothers out of there—before some cartel kills or kidnaps them.

His gaze focused on a group of girls he knew from his old neighborhood. Among them, he saw Nelly waltzing down the beach. Her long black hair flowed out behind her in the strong breeze. Toro heard her laughter and watched as her bare feet danced in and out of the waves.

Sexy, was the first thought that came to his mind, followed by, *When did little Nelly become so sexy?* He watched until she passed by and disappeared in the distance.

❦

A week later, Toro met with friends at the beach to play soccer. There was Nelly again, watching from the pier above. Distracted, he didn't notice the soccer ball until it smacked him on the forehead and sent him sprawling backward.

"Pay attention, man!" his buddy, Alfonso, said, helping him to his feet. "You can talk to her later."

"Don't know what you're talking about, dude," Toro replied, regaining his composure.

After the game, Toro got up his nerve and strolled toward Nelly. Carlos, the eighteen-year-old son of a local hotel owner approached first. Toro heard him asking her out.

Damn! That punk Carlos. He's an arrogant, worthless daddy's-boy. She deserves better. I should talk to her. Nah...I better wait.

Toro couldn't stop thinking about Nelly, so he sought the perfect time to approach her. He waited for days...which seemed like weeks.

Asking friends, he discovered she worked in a BBQ place in Villa Caliente, the neighboring town, just ten minutes away. Suddenly hungry for barbecued chicken, he jumped on the rickety local bus and arrived near closing time.

"Hey, Nelly," he said.

"Hola, Toro."

"I'd like a chicken taco and cold beer ...please."

He kept his eyes on Nelly while trying to act uninterested. He watched her cleaning tables and preparing to finish her shift. *She's a looker. I remember how she used to play hopscotch with her sister,*

Lupita in the park—her long hair in pig-tails and a smile on her face.

Toro handed her twenty pesos to pay for the food. He took a deep breath. "It looks like your shift is almost over. Do you want to catch a bus back to La Perlita with me?"

"Sure. Just let me tell my boss I'm leaving."

Toro nodded, hiding his smile.

"How long have you worked here?" he asked a few minutes later, as they stood on the street waiting for the bus.

"A month."

He hesitated. "Do you go out much?"

"No."

The bus arrived, saving Toro from more small talk. As they sat side-by-side, Nelly gazed out the right side of the bus while Toro watched her reflection in the window. When their eyes met, he smiled. He noticed her tuck a loose strand of hair behind her ear and noted the dimple in her left cheek. *Say something!* No words formed.

When the bus stopped at the entrance to the Barrio where Nelly lived, she thanked Toro for his company and stepped off the bus.

He watched her walk away. *Damn. Why does she make me so tongue-tied?*

෴

Toro knew he was not the only one interested in beautiful, raven-haired Nelly. And his rival, Carlos, had a car and money.

Toro waited for the right opportunity to make his next move. That opportunity presented itself a few days later during a beach birthday party for Nelly's eighteen-year-old sister, Lupita.

While sitting with Alfonso and other friends on the pier, analyzing the town soccer team's loss that day, he noticed Nelly walking toward the party. She looked enticing in a red tank top and denim shorts.

"What did you think about that last goal?" Alfonso asked, staring at Toro.

"Um, which goal?" Toro stammered. Hesitating for a few seconds, he took a deep breath and jumped to his feet with bravado. Before he could take a step forward, Carlos appeared out of nowhere and took Nelly's hand.

Damn! Toro watched in dismay as the two set off away from the party and down the beach.

He followed, hiding behind large rocks and the thatch roof, *palapa*, restaurants that lined the shoreline. He could see Nelly glance behind her as if sensing someone was following.

Toro's anger surged when he saw Carlos push her against the back wall of a restaurant and kiss her forcibly. He watched Nelly struggle to get away.

Stepping out from behind a boulder, he approached. "Get your hands off her Carlos!"

Nelly used Toro's sudden appearance to push away from Carlos. She wiped her mouth and took a step forward.

"What are *you* doing here?" Carlos asked, with clenched jaw.

Toro responded with more confidence than he felt. "I'd wager Nelly prefers my company to yours, so take your hands off her," he said coolly.

Carlos stepped toward Toro—his hands curled into fists. "Oh, yeah?"

But Toro had an advantage. Standing six feet tall, with broad shoulders, he looked down at Carlos. "Yeah, *cabron*. You want to mess with me, rich boy?"

Nelly intervened, standing between the two macho teens. Toro noticed her body tremble as if in fear. "Toro is right, Carlos. I don't want to be with you anymore." With that, she moved to stand next to Toro.

Toro steeled his body, ready to fight—daring Carlos to make the first move.

Neither boy moved.

Neither blinked.

"Take her then!" Carlos spat on the ground and marched away.

"Thank you for saving me from him, Toro," Nelly said a few moments later as they stood together on the sand.

Toro kept his eyes on Carlos, making sure he was leaving the party. He clenched and unclenched his fists. *I should have smashed him to a pulp.*

He realized Nelly had said something. "What?" he finally asked, turning in her direction.

"Thank you for being here for me."

Toro looked down into her dark gentle eyes. "Of course."

"Carlos had never been that aggressive before."

Toro lost himself in her eyes.

"Why did it take you so long to say something?" she asked.

"I wasn't sure you were interested. I thought maybe you liked that jerk." He took a deep breath and exhaled as if he'd just climbed a tall mountain and reached the top.

"I've liked you for a long time, Toro. I didn't think you liked me that way. Like...as more than just a friend." She gently touched his hand and smiled.

Though her hand barely grazed his, the sensation lingered, captivating Toro's heart.

"But you need to know, I'm only fourteen. My parents won't let me date you...or anybody," she said, a sad smile slipping into place.

Toro took her hands into his. "It's not about age. It's about how we feel. We'll figure it out."

≪

The young couple met every afternoon, hiding their relationship from Nelly's family. Nelly knew her father would not allow her to be alone with a boy at her age, and her mother, Lidia, would agree with whatever her father decided.

But people were starting to put two-and-two together about them, including Nelly's older brother, Ruben. He'd heard the rumors and warned his sister, "Watch out. I've seen him around town at night. He likes drinking and partying. He has no family, lives in a rented room, and has obviously no plans to get an education or do anything good with his life."

"Who are you to judge, Ruben? And all boys in La Perlita drink and party. What else is there to do here? What are you doing with *your* life? You're not in school. You get drunk every weekend and smoke dope. You never listen to anything Mamá or Papá tell you."

She could see his body tense.

"That may be true, little sis, but I want more for you. And he's not it," he snapped.

❧CHAPTER SIX❧

N elly ignored Ruben. She thought of Toro day and night. Meeting him in secret became both exciting and dangerous.

She loved the tingling sensations running through her body when he kissed her and the comfort she felt when they held hands walking through the dense banana orchards.

Her threats to tell her parents about Ruben's drinking and smoking were enough to keep him silent, but she had to be careful her parents didn't find out any other way—especially her father—or she'd be banned from seeing Toro. Living without Toro and his kisses was something her fourteen-year-old heart couldn't bear.

Every Sunday, Nelly went to Mass with her family and prayed to *La Virgin María*. "Help me be a good, proper, girl," she whispered, with head bowed. "And, give me the strength to ask my parents to allow us to date."

On a warm February evening, in their secret hiding place near the lagoon, Toro held Nelly in his arms. Her hair smelled of vanilla and her lips tasted like cherries. Her skin felt as smooth as silk and his caresses brought sighs from her throat. After a few moments, he stepped back an inch and closed his hands around her hips, savoring her firm, feminine shape. "I love you, Nelly. Let's run off together."

Nelly reached up, put her arms around his neck and looked into his eyes. She then nestled her head on his chest. "I love you too, but we should wait."

"Wait for what?" he asked, impatience resonating in his voice.

Nelly put space between them. "We've only been dating for eight-and-a-half weeks, Toro. I'm barely fourteen. Can't we wait?" she asked, looking into his dark, brooding eyes.

Toro exhaled. "Not for long, Princess," he said. He caressed her shoulders and planted kisses on her neck.

༚

Two days later, Toro's mother called—crying. "Son, your father's drinking is out of control. And...he's become even more violent."

He heard her hold back a sob. His anger surged.

"I'm afraid. I'm embarrassed to tell you. But he's slapping and punching me almost every day now. Please help."

Toro's chest expanded in a rage he hadn't felt for years. "I'll do something, Mamá. I promise."

He snapped the phone shut and rushed to meet Nelly for their planned rendezvous by the lagoon. "I love you, Nelly," he said, holding her close moments later. "But I have to go. I get paid tomorrow. I'll leave for Michoacán on the midnight bus."

"What's happening, Toro?"

He hesitated, embarrassed to share family secrets. *I need to tell her. If she cares about me, she'll understand.* "I thought my father had stopped drinking so much...or at least my mom wasn't the

42

target of his anger," he said. "But she says it's getting worse. I don't know what to do, but I have to do something."

Nelly looked up into Toro's dark, sad eyes. "Please don't leave."

"I have to." *I used to feel so helpless when he hurt her. I'm not helpless now.* "If you love me, sneak out of your house tonight and leave with me tomorrow."

He saw the panic in Nelly's eyes and waited. Her body tensed in his arms, and he knew a battle was raging in her mind. *Please say yes.*

"Okay," she blurted.

⤸

Sneaking out of her house on that dark Friday evening in February, Nelly circled the privacy wall of the American woman's house under construction next door. Her heart beat in fear that her parents would catch her. *I can't lose him. I can't live without him.* She ran to the lagoon to embrace her destiny.

That night, obeying the feelings in her body and choosing to ignore the logic in her mind, Nelly spent the night in Toro's tiny, rented room.

⤳

Hours later, in the early morning, she dressed and left Toro's bed to hurry home. She could still feel his kisses and smell his cologne on her hands. Although wanting to savor the love they'd found in each other's arms the night before, she knew she had to face her parents and say goodbye.

Maybe Papá has left to go fishing.

43

Maybe they overslept and don't even know I'm not in my bedroom.

The closer she got to her house, the higher her anxiety level grew.

Oh, no. The lights are on. Somebody's awake!

Maybe it's just Mamá making tortillas. She'll understand.

Will she?

Nelly turned the front door knob and found it locked.

Maybe I'll just leave without my things and without saying goodbye.

No, I can't do that.

She knocked lightly.

Her father opened the door, looked at his nervous, wide-eyed daughter and with a stone face, said, "Whoever you were with last night—you're his now."

"But, Papá!" she cried.

"Ruben says you've been sneaking around with Enrique's son, Toro. Well, you're his to clothe and feed now. Get your stuff. Go!"

Nelly looked to her mother for emotional support, but found none. She and Toro had taken the risk, and both knew the consequences. Toro *le habia robado*, had stolen her virginity, and she could not return home. Nelly was now a woman and belonged to Toro.

Nelly stuffed her brush, hair ties, face creams, and a few clothes into an old pillowcase, grabbed her stuffed fluffy-white rabbit and hugged her mother. "I'm going to Michoacán with Toro. Please don't hate me."

She watched the tears fall from her mother's eyes.

Nelly turned and yelled at her father. "You're a hypocrite, Papá. I've heard the family stories. You took off with Mamá when she was my age, so why are you so angry with me and Toro?"

Her father turned his back and walked to the back patio, slamming the door behind him.

Lidia opened the door and followed him, not saying a word.

Wiping the tears from her eyes, Nelly left her childhood home and went to meet Toro at the corner store, as she had so many times before.

Toro's heart constricted to see such sadness in Nelly's face as she approached. "Are you okay?" he asked gathering her close.

Her bottom lip trembled. "No, but I will be."

The young couple strolled away, hand in hand for all to see.

"We'll leave tonight," Toro said gently, caressing Nelly's hand as they walked back to his living quarters. "I have the bus tickets. We'll be in Michoacán by morning."

"Are you sure we have to do this?" she asked, reeling from her father's scorn and wondering if she'd done the right thing in leaving her family for Toro.

Toro kicked an empty coke can on the ground. "I have to protect my mother and brothers. I can't just stay here and let my father abuse them. If he's beating my mother every day, my brothers will soon be in his crosshairs, if they aren't already.

"I've been on my own for almost three years, Nelly, without family. You're my family now, and I don't care what your parents or anybody else says. We'll make our life work, together. But first, let's go help my mom."

Nelly stopped and put her arms around Toro's waist, holding him close. Looking up into his eyes, she whispered, "I will always love you, Toro Rivera. Forever and ever."

❧CHAPTER SEVEN❧

Toro held Nelly's hand, enjoying the feel of her head resting on his shoulder as the Primer Plus Bus Line took them closer and closer to the state of Michoacán.

"What will we do when we get there?" Nelly asked, snuggling close.

Toro stared out the window, lost in thought. He'd been going over his options in his head. "The first thing is to stop my father from beating on Mamá or my brothers. Enough is enough. My family has suffered under his short temper and drinking way too long."

"How will you do that?"

"I don't know. But I'll do what I have to do."

Sleep eluded Toro as he held Nelly close. They snuggled under a light blanket and whispered, not wanting to wake the other passengers.

"How long do you think we'll be in Santana?" Nelly asked, raising her head from Toro's shoulder to look into his face.

"I'm hoping just a few days—but we'll stay as long as needed. I don't know how to stop my father from drinking...or how to get him to control his anger. Maybe my *Tio* Juan can help."

Nelly laid her head on Toro's chest, intoxicated by the smell of his cologne. "And, when we get back to La Perlita...where are we going to live?" she asked, already planning the rest of her life.

"I can't think so far ahead, *amorcita*. Let's see what happens here first. Try to get some sleep. We'll be there at sunrise."

Nelly smiled as she drifted off to sleep. She loved it when Toro called her sweetheart.

⌘

As arranged, Toro's Uncle Juan met them at the bus station in Los Reyes. The house was still ninety minutes away in the Santana hills, and he'd offered to drive them.

"Nephew, it's good to see you again so soon," Juan said, clasping Toro's hands in his. "And...who is this beautiful young girl you've brought with you?"

"Tio, Nelly is my girlfriend. Nelly, this is my Tio Juan, my dad's older brother."

"You've done well for yourself, *Sobrino*." Juan punched his nephew on the shoulder as they made their way to his black pickup truck. "Welcome to the Rivera family, little Nelly."

"So, Tio, what's with this fancy Ram 4x4 truck? You've never been able to afford such an expensive vehicle...ever."

"Times are better."

"It looks like it, but I was just here four months ago and they weren't this good," Toro said.

Juan hesitated, looked in the rear view mirror at Nelly nestled in the back seat and then at Toro, riding shotgun.

"You can speak freely, Tio. Nelly knows what's happening with the cartels. I filled her in on the bus—at least what I know."

"Well, we harvested a good crop two months ago. We gave a portion to the Valencia cartel enforcers and sold the rest. We made enough between your father and me to pull ourselves up a notch and buy things we've never been able to afford—and we sent money to your grandparents and your Uncle Leo in Morelia."

"That sounds like quite a profit, Tio."

"It'd be a lot better if we didn't have to hand over so much to the cartel."

Toro looked out the window, trying to enjoy the familiar view. "Who did you hire for the harvest?"

"Esteben and Julio are supervising some local boys we think we can trust. If we ever find out we can't trust them, the cartel assures us they will take care of them."

Toro's head snapped toward his uncle. "What? Papá promised that Esteben and Julio would not participate in this drug mess, Tio. And now you tell me they're supervising the harvest?"

"Wake up, Toro. This is serious business. We keep it in the family. We need managers we trust to not steal or rat us out to the *Federales*."

Toro swallowed his anger while feeling acid in the pit of his stomach. He added this news to the list of things to discuss with his father. "You said you paid the Valencia Cartel. Why? I heard La Familia organization is in charge here now."

"It goes back and forth. One day we hear the Valencias are in charge and then we hear they've been pushed out by La Familia,"

Juan said. "We hope it's true that the Valencias are gone and won't be back for any more of our crops."

"How do you keep safe, Tio?"

"We don't choose sides. We're just farmers. I do know citizens are fed up with the drugs and related crime though, which is helping La Familia organization increase in numbers. The leaders are serious about getting the Valencias out of the entire state of Michoacán. Them and *all* cartels. And, at least here in our county, the Valencias seem to be gone."

"So La Familia are the good guys in this?"

"That's how it looks. Their propaganda says they're common workers united to end oppression and humiliation by people in power. They're no longer willing to see the people of Michoacán trampled upon."

Toro opened the window and breathed in the fresh mountain air. "It's about time somebody stood up against the rich, powerful and corrupt."

"Well, like I said, right now La Familia is in charge—at least around this part of the state."

"Do you trust them?" Toro asked.

"I don't trust anybody. But, we'll see. Their leader, *El Mas Loco,* seems to run the group with an iron hand. He carries a 'bible' with his own writings on morality. They plan to eliminate crystal meth trafficking and other narcotics, along with the kidnapping, extortion, and highway assaults."

"All of that has been happening here?" Nelly asked.

Hearing the fear in her voice, Toro looked to the back seat and smiled. "Don't worry. You'll be safe. And we'll be in and out of here as soon as we can."

"It's starting to happen all over Mexico, Nelly," Juan said. "The number of cartels is growing and they're trying to eliminate each other to pick up supply routes. We're just farmers trying to keep our heads down and make some money."

"What do the locals say?" Toro asked.

"Everybody wants to believe in La Familia. I've heard good and bad. They're putting money into building schools and churches. They've built drainage systems in some towns. And they've even opened drug rehab centers."

"What's the bad, Tio?"

"That, just like the Valencias, they have the police on their payroll so there's no official authority to go to with complaints. Added to that, La Familia will torture and kill you if you're involved with a cartel. They're scary. They torture, kill, and extort in the name of reform. Then they pray and donate to charity."

Nelly patted Toro's shoulder. "Are you sure we can go back to La Perlita soon? I don't think we should be here too long."

"*Sí, amor.* We'll leave as soon as we can."

Toro shut his window and returned his attention to Juan. "So, what began as a small group of armed men here in Michoacán trying to protect their children from meth and crime has turned into a major vigilante group?"

"You got it. What's important right now is that La Familia has chased the Valencias out of this area. And, they are ignoring the marijuana crops as long as we give them a cut. I don't agree with all the killing, but growing marijuana for profit sits right with me.

"So, to answer your original question, Toro, rather than paying the Valencias, we'll now be paying La Familia...for protection."

Toro struggled with the change happening in his home state—the Valencias, La Familia, My family.

֍

Thirty minutes out of Los Reyes, Juan swore under his breath and slowed the car as they approached a military checkpoint. He pulled the vehicle to the side of the road, following the impatient hand motions of four government soldiers dressed in dark green fatigues.

Looking out the backseat window, Nelly noticed the soldiers seemed barely out of their teens. The machine guns they held close to their chests worried her. "What do they want?" she asked.

Toro lowered his window as two of the soldiers approached his side of the truck.

"Where ya headed?" a young soldier asked, looking into the vehicle.

"To Santana," Toro replied.

"What's in the bundles there in the back?"

"Just clothes and personal items. We'll be visiting family for a few days."

"Step out of the vehicle," a soldier with a scar on his left cheek demanded.

Nelly felt her hands start to shake. *Hadn't Toro and Juan just been talking about highway assaults and kidnappings?*

Toro, out of the car first, opened the door and helped Nelly out, holding on to her hand.

Juan followed, and the three stood together, watching.

"What are they looking for, Toro?" Nelly whispered, wishing she was safe at home with her parents.

"Drugs, guns, ammunition...I guess. We have nothing to be worried about." Toro pulled her close.

After checking under and throughout the vehicle, the military boys allowed them to leave.

Juan let out his breath as they drove away. "Damn. That was close. It's a good thing they didn't look under the seat and find my revolver."

"Your what?" Toro gasped.

"It's in a secret compartment under the seat. For protection."

"You could have gotten us all arrested, Tio!"

Juan held up his cell phone. "They would have just detained us, until your father or one of your brothers came to pay for our release. They're only a phone call away."

"Why...why do you need protection?" Nelly asked.

"You never know who the enemy is or who's coming at you, Nelly. It's against the law to possess more than one small gun, which you are required to register with the army and keep at home. That's just insane in today's Mexico. I don't travel without it. I'd rather break the stupid law than be dead."

Exhausted and scared, Nelly snuggled under her blanket and prayed silently to the Virgin Mary for forgiveness—for her sins, for disobeying her parent's wishes, and for giving herself to Toro.

And, as she started another prayer asking La Virgin to keep them safe, she nodded off to sleep.

ᚙCHAPTER EIGHTᚙ

Juan, Toro, and Nelly arrived at the Rivera home in time for breakfast.

Toro closed the passenger door behind him and opened Nelly's door. His mother and siblings came running from the house and surrounded him with greetings of joy and hugs. *How nice to be home.*

Juan waved and drove off to his own house down the dusty road.

Finishing the group hug, Toro motioned for Nelly. "Mamá, this is my girlfriend, Nelly."

Maria's expression changed to one of confusion. "*¿Qué?*"

Esteben and Julio weren't confused at all and congratulated their brother with back slaps, whoops, and high fives.

"Hey, Nelly. I never thought I'd see you here," Esteben said, remembering his grade school crush.

"*Hola*, Esteben."

Nelly approached Toro's mother and shook her hand. "*Hola, Señora*. I remember you from the Barrio. I'm the daughter of Lidia Sanchez and Roberto Gonzales."

"*Sí*, I remember you now. You've grown up since I last saw you, Nelly. How are your parents?"

"Not happy with us at the moment," Toro interjected, as he escorted Nelly into the kitchen. "She can tell you about it later. I'm hungry. Where's Papá?"

"He's sleeping off last night's binge," Esteben said, evident anger in his voice.

Toro noticed a bruise on his mom's right upper arm. "I'm here, Mamá."

Maria let out an audible sigh, wiped a tear from her cheek, and focused on the task at hand—feeding her eldest son and his girlfriend.

The moment the chopped onions, garlic and cilantro sizzled in the hot saucepan, a red-eyed, disheveled Enrique strode into the kitchen. "*Café*," he demanded.

"Good morning, Papá," Toro said, sitting down across from his father.

Nelly hurried to the coffeepot, grabbed two mugs from the dish drainer and served Toro and his father hot black coffee. Returning the pot to its place, she asked, "Señora, how can I help?"

"You can get me eggs out of the fridge and then make some tortillas," she said, and watched Nelly rush to do as asked.

Maria turned to her younger sons. "Esteben and Julio, take your brothers outside so Toro and your father can visit."

"*Si, Mamá.*"

"So, what brought you back here so soon, Hijo?" Enrique asked as Toro's brothers hurried outside with their soccer ball. "And tell me about this beautiful girl you brought with you."

"Well, the short version is that Nelly and I are in love and her parents wouldn't let us be together, so we came here," Toro lied, not wanting to mention his mother's phone call.

Enrique poured milk into his coffee. "And what do you expect to do here?"

"Get a job—maybe in construction if I can find work in Santana."

"Well, if you're staying for a while, I can use your help in the fields. There's no reason to run off into town to get a job."

Toro noticed his father's eyes moving up and down Nelly's slim figure as she set plates of scrambled eggs and sausage on the table. He willed himself to stay put and not strike out.

Nelly placed a stack of warm tortillas in front of Toro and then took her own breakfast outside, following Maria.

A few moments later, Maria and Nelly sat in silence outside the back door.

Maria watched her four youngest sons kick a soccer ball around the backyard, and her heart filled with love. "What happened back in La Perlita?" she finally asked, sipping freshly made mango juice.

"Toro and I fell in love in December. We wanted to be together. I knew my parents wouldn't let me date him, so we kept it a secret." Nelly shifted in her chair and set her juice on the ground. "But, after your phone call, we ran off—and here we are. Toro worries about you and wanted to help. I hope I won't be a bother."

"No. Of course not. I'll enjoy having another woman here. With my husband and four boys—now five with Toro—and the new one to come, I appreciate the company."

"Toro told me you were pregnant. If I may ask, how far along are you?"

"This baby is due within the next few weeks. Did Toro tell you the doctor says I'm having another boy?"

Nelly smiled. "Yes, he did. Congratulations."

"I turned thirty-one last month and I'm having my sixth son," Maria said, shaking her head. "I still can't believe how life turned out for me."

Nelly watched Maria grimacing and moving around in her chair to get comfortable. "Can I help you with something Señora?" she asked.

"No, I'll be okay. I'll be glad when this baby is out of my stomach and into my arms, though. Will you two stay long?"

"It's up to Toro. Where he goes, I go. I don't think we'll leave until he feels you are safe. My parents know I was coming here with Toro. I didn't leave without telling them...even if my father was angry. I'm only fourteen and he's overly protective."

"I'm glad they know where you are. Toro must love you to settle down at sixteen."

"Yes, we love each other. I hope my parents will understand."

Maria stared off across the yard. "Over time, parents forgive young couples who run off with the one they love—even if it's against their wishes. You know, we want our children to have a better life than we've had."

Maria clapped when Julio scored a goal against his older brother, Esteben. "Those boys play soccer every chance they get. Did you know Toro wanted to play professional soccer?"

"No. He's never mentioned it," Nelly said.

Maria and Nelly sat in silence for a while. "My sons are my life. They make everything else worthwhile," Maria said quietly.

❧

Toro finished his coffee and sat back in his chair, with arms crossed. "Papá, I want to talk to you about something. Tio Juan mentioned that Esteben and Julio are supervising the marijuana harvest. You told me you wouldn't involve them. But apparently they are involved."

"It's not your business, Hijo," Enrique said.

Toro's anger surged. "It is my business," he shouted. "They're my brothers. You want them to think drug growing is an honorable profession?"

Face full of anger, Enrique stumbled from his chair and raised his fisted hand to Toro.

Unafraid, Toro grabbed his father's wrist and forced him back into the chair. Standing over him, he snapped, "Don't you dare, you coward! You think you can keep abusing everyone? You think there's no one to stop you? Well, there is now."

Hearing the commotion, Nelly and Maria rushed into the kitchen to find Enrique slumped in his chair, arms crossed, staring at Toro.

Toro took deep breaths to control his anger. "The next time you raise your hand to hit my mother or my brothers, I will hurt you! Do you understand? It stops now!" With that, he stormed out, slamming the screen door behind him.

"Don't you threaten me!" his father yelled at Toro's back.

Nelly and Maria looked at each other and ran after Toro.

ᚙCHAPTER NINE᚜

Toro and Nelly had been at the Rivera home just over a month when Maria gave birth to her sixth son. Nelly, along with Juan's wife, Lupe, helped bring the black-haired, crying baby into the world.

"He's a tiny little thing, Mamá," Toro said, looking into the face of his newest brother, Jesus Antonio, a few hours later.

Nelly stood next to him and caressed the baby's face.

"Tiny, just like you were, Son, and look at you now. Nearly seventeen, tall and strong like a bull, with a temper to match your father's."

Toro knew his mother was referring to the heated arguments he'd had with his father over the last few weeks—standing up to him each time he lashed out in drunken anger. *I no longer fear him. He's a drunken bully, used to getting his way. No more!*

Toro nodded, remembering the pivotal incidence two weeks earlier, when his father fell over a tree root in the backyard. Toro found him passed out with a bruise on his forehead, vomit on his shirt and urine on his pants. He used the water hose to wake him.

"Is this who you want to be, Papá?" he'd asked. "An old dried-up, fallen-down drunk despised by everybody?"

His father had begun to cry. Toro helped him shower and change clothes before the family returned from the store.

Toro handed the baby to Nelly. "Well, enough of this sissy stuff. I need to get back and help Esteben and Julio prune the vines."

᷾

A month later, Toro, his Uncle Juan, and his father gathered in the front yard after a long day's work. Acknowledging the unspoken peace agreement with his dad, Toro spoke with respect. "I still think this pot growing is a dangerous business, Papá. I don't want my brothers involved, arrested, and sent to jail."

Enrique sat back in his chair and dusted off his work boots. "It has its risks, Hijo, but we can't let that stop us. As I told you before, we have to keep this in the family. Your uncle and I can't do this alone."

Juan stood up to enter the house. "You two want beers?"

"I'll take a cold Coke, *Hermano*," Enrique said, looking at his eldest son.

"I'll have a beer, Tio. Thanks," Toro replied. *It's been much nicer without my dad's drinking. I hope he can keep this up.*

Toro measured his words. "I've been thinking, Papá. Let Esteben and Julio work with the fruit trees and vegetables. There's plenty to keep them busy there. I'll work with you and Tio and even manage the marijuana crops."

His father sat up straight. "You're willing to stay and do this?" he asked, surprise mixed with delight radiating in his face.

"Yes. For a time, to see how it goes." Toro hated the words coming out of his mouth, but he'd laid awake night after night thinking about his family's situation. He could not force them to sell the farm and move. He found it ironic he was asking his father to do the same thing his father had asked his grandfather to do so many years earlier.

The pot sales were bringing in good money to lift them out of poverty and the La Familia organization was keeping the area safe from the cartels vying for the rich growing lands of Michoacán. The best way he knew to ensure his brother's safety was to take over the marijuana crop management so they would be out of danger. *I'll stay on for a year, put aside some money, and when Uncle Juan's sons are older, I'll take my brothers and leave.*

"I've been asking around in town," he told his father. "It seems the Federales have become experts at spotting crops from their helicopters. After this month's harvest, we need to move the plants out from between the vegetables and concentrate the planting under the canopy of trees on the hillside."

"How much area is that?" Juan asked, plopping himself into a chair and handing Toro a cold bottle of Tecate.

"I walked it today. We have about half a soccer-field-size area to hide the plants."

Juan shook his head. "That will cut into our profits."

"I talked to a buyer when I went into Los Reyes a few days ago," Toro said. "The current rate is $4,000 for that amount of pot.

That's after paying La Familia their cut. With proper water and fertilizer we can harvest a crop every three months."

"That's $16,000 a year," his father said, smiling. "We've only been able to get half that amount of yield up 'til now. And not at that price."

Toro finished his beer. "Well, if we're taking the risk, we need to do it right and better."

"So you're on board, Sobrino?" Juan asked.

Toro saw the surprise on his uncle's face. "Yep. And I'll have the workers clear another similar-sized area on the north side of the property. Within three months we can double production."

"Just curious, Hijo. What made you change your mind?"

Toro checked the numbers he'd jotted down on a napkin. "I did the math. I get paid $280.00 a month working construction in La Perlita. That's $850.00 every three months. With the three of us dividing $4,000 after each harvest, my cut would be $1,300 for the same three months. When the second parcel is producing, we'll get double. I'd be bringing in $2,600 rather than $850.00. For me, it makes sense."

"Then let's toast to a better future," Enrique said with a smile, lifting his coke bottle. "*Salud!*"

"*Salud!*" Juan replied.

"To a bright and *prosperous* future," Toro countered, resigned to his plan of action.

⌁

"I want to go home," Nelly whispered to Toro one late night in December as they lay in bed. "We've been here ten months. I miss my family, the seashore, and my life there. Your dad isn't drinking anymore and he hardly ever hits your mom. Can we leave soon? And be home by Christmas?"

"We'll go soon, amorcita," Toro replied. "I want to leave, too."

Nelly turned to face him with a smile. "Seriously? What about the 'one-year plan' you told me about?"

"I thought I could stay on for a full year, but I'm ready to leave."

He kissed Nelly on the forehead. "The guy in Los Reyes who buys our marijuana is arranging a deal where his group will process the family crops and I'll sell some of it down in La Perlita. He buys from lots of growers, so the product is plentiful."

"You were always against this, Toro. Then you started to manage the harvest for your dad and now you're talking about selling drugs back in La Perlita. What changed for you?" she asked, her delight now reflecting concern.

"Whether we like it or not, people are growing and selling marijuana, Nelly. There's a huge demand. I can make more money in three months doing this than I can make a year in construction. I'll only sell a bit here and there. Just enough to give us an okay life."

"Just a little bit?"

"Yes, just so we can pay our bills," he said. "And selling isn't as dangerous as growing."

"What do you mean it's not as dangerous?"

"Even though we've hidden our crops under trees, we're still at risk of getting caught."

"Like how?" Nelly asked, alarmed.

"I heard armed soldiers marched through farms in southern Michoacán last week. A local farmer says *Federales* in a small plane flying overhead radioed down GPS coordinates for a suspected pot patch. The soldiers were there within minutes destroying the fields. They pulled up six-foot-high plants by the roots and burned them! The farmers were in the midst of harvesting the crop moments before the soldiers arrived."

"Oh, my gosh! What happened to the farmers and their workers?"

"They fled, but most were found and hauled off. The soldiers shot those who resisted. That's why I don't want my brothers involved. They're just kids. My dad and uncle can take the risk or stop growing. The federal government is on a mission to hunt, find and destroy. I want us out of here."

"But your dad and uncle can't stop growing, Toro. You told me they'll be killed if they don't obey the cartel orders."

Toro took a deep breath. "That was before, when the Valencia cartel was in charge here. La Familia is taking a cut, but not pressuring the farmers to grow."

"I can't keep this all straight, Toro. But you've changed. It scares me."

"I don't like it either, but it's the reality of life. We can choose poverty or choose to make money and have a better life. Selling pot is less dangerous than this."

Given the dangers of where that "better life" could lead them, a part of Nelly wished she'd never run away with Toro. It was too late now. "Who will you sell to in La Perlita?"

"The gringos that fill the town from November through April each year. In fact, I'm sure they're there right now, wondering how to get some good weed."

Nelly sat up in bed. "So...we can go home soon?"

"Yes. We'll be home for Christmas."

"Well, then, I want to give you an early Christmas present."

"What would that be?" Toro said, flashing Nelly a sexy smile and motioning for her to lie back down beside him.

"I'm pregnant."

"Pregnant! Great! It's about time."

Toro's smile widened and his heart warmed. *It's a good thing there will be more money coming in. I'm going to be a father.* He kissed Nelly and let his passion show her how much this news meant to him.

ᖇCHAPTER TENᖆ

Toro and Nelly packed their belongings a few days later and said their goodbyes over breakfast.

"I've told you I'm against you taking Esteben, Julio, and Miguel with you," Enrique said. "What am I going to do about workers?"

"There are plenty of guys around Santana looking for work, Papá," Esteben said, setting his pillowcase full of clothes by the front door and placing his soccer ball on top.

"And like I told you yesterday," Toro added, "Tio Juan's older sons are ready to leave middle school and work in the harvest. I think they have their eyes on the money and all the cell phones, stereos, and video games they'll be able to buy."

Enrique grunted, left the table, and stormed out the back door without another word.

Maria's eyes filled with tears as she hugged Esteben, Julio, and Miguel, and then watched them toss their belongings into the back of Juan's truck.

Toro held his mother tight against his chest. He knew her sadness—they'd sat at the kitchen table the previous night and talked for hours while the others slept. They'd gone over the pros and cons of taking his brothers with him—the pros being they'd be out of harm's way of the Federales, cartels, and his father, but the big con was that she would be more vulnerable to her husband's unpredictable temper. And they ran the risk that Enrique might take Ricky out of elementary school and put him to work in the fields.

The pros had won.

"Take Esteben to the clinic when you get to La Perlita. They have had a file on him since birth. He's not growing. See if they have growth hormones or something they can give him."

"I will Mamá," Toro promised.

"And get Miguel into the Barrio middle school right after the holidays. He only has one more semester before graduating."

"I will. I promise."

"Any instructions on Julio?" Toro asked, teasing his mother.

"Yes. Watch out for him. He tells the girls he's Mario Lopez' twin brother and they swoon all over him."

"Which Mario Lopez?" Nelly asked, confused.

"Mario Lopez on television. The young actor," Maria explained.

Nelly laughed. "Well, he does kinda look like him," she said.

Hugging Maria one last time, Nelly stroked Ricky's curly dark hair, and followed Toro to Juan's truck.

As they drove off, Toro watched his mother from the side rear-view mirror until they reached the main road and she was out of his sight. As a soon-to-be father, with the responsibility to care for Nelly and three of his brothers, he could not look back. The future lay before him. Unknown. Inevitable. He took a deep breath, let it out, and settled in for the trip to Los Reyes.

"Thanks for the ride, Tio," Toro said, shaking Juan's calloused hand at the bus depot a couple of hours later. "Please take care of my mom and little brothers."

"I will, Sobrino. You take care, too."

"Listen, my dad isn't drinking now. That needs to continue. If that changes, call me. And if he takes Ricky out of school, I want to know that, too."

"I got it. It's best for me he doesn't drink. I need him alert and working."

"Okay, then. You be safe, Tio."

"We plan to be." Juan looked around to make sure they were alone. "We'll be buying a half dozen rifles and some AK-47s with profits from the next harvest," he said. "We're planning on La Familia keeping us safe. But just in case they can't, we'll protect our own."

"This whole drug thing is insane, you know?" Toro said, shaking his head. "Thousands of our people are dying, families are torn apart, honest farmers are breaking the law...all of this so rich Americans can snort cocaine, kill their brain cells with meth, and smoke weed!"

"It's not just the rich, Nephew. All those crazy gringos in the north love this stuff. It's supply and demand. Drug growing and smuggling is a billion dollar industry. Stop feeling guilty about making money."

Toro's gaze followed Nelly and his brothers entering the bus station. "I'm working on that 'stop feeling guilty' thing, Tio. This is against all I've ever believed, so it's not that easy."

"Get real, Toro. Stop being such an idiot. Do you want to work hard for the rest of your life and only earn enough to buy rice and beans? You have a child on the way. Do you want to raise your child the way you grew up...with nothing? This is a chance to get out of poverty. And, you're not forcing anybody to buy the drugs. You're just the supplier."

Toro hesitated. He had asked himself those same questions over the last several weeks, wrestling with his decision. He had Nelly and three of his brothers to support, and a baby on the way. It was time to 'man up' and take charge of his own life.

"You're right, Tio. You're right."

❧CHAPTER ELEVEN❧

T oro jumped off the bus and breathed in the fresh ocean air of La Perlita. *Home.*

Nelly woke up Esteben, Julio, and Miguel. She smoothed her hair and stepped off the bus with a smile on her face.

Toro watched Esteben, Julio, and Miguel scurry down the bus steps and look around—smiles on their faces. It had been four years since his younger brothers had set foot in La Perlita. He wondered if they still considered this home.

The weary group left their belongings with the reservations agent at the bus station and asked around town for available rentals. By noon they had moved their few possessions into a small two-bedroom house in the Barrio, a few blocks from Nelly's family home.

With half of the pesos in his pocket, Toro paid the deposit and first month's rent to the landlord and handed the keys to Nelly. "Esteben and Julio," he said, "come with me. We'll take the local bus into Villa Caliente and order some furniture. Miguel, help Nelly clean." He dug into his pocket again. "Nelly, here's some money for food. Load up the cupboards and don't forget to buy beer. We'll be back in a few hours."

A bit later, Nelly sang a soft melody as she folded their clothes and laid them in empty cardboard boxes from the corner store. She placed her brush, hair ties, and beauty products on the back of the toilet in the tiny bathroom. "Our first home," she said to her fluffy-white rabbit, putting him on top of her clothes box. "You'll have a proper place to sit once we have some furniture."

❧

Toro and his brothers arrived at the house before sunset, in the back of the furniture company delivery truck. They hopped out of the back of the truck and began lowering a kitchen table, chairs, sofa and love seat, a chest of drawers and mattresses.

With the furniture in place, Toro held Nelly close at his side and surveyed their first home. "It's not much, but it's a start," he said.

"I love it, Toro," Nelly said with a big smile on her face.

Later that night, Toro snuggled with Nelly on their new double-sized mattress. He could hear his three brothers breathing deeply in their room across the hall. Toro tried to relax, but the weight of responsibility threatened to overwhelm him. *I'm seventeen. I need to act like I know what I'm doing. But what am I doing?* His new life, as head of his own household, had begun.

❧

The following afternoon, the four Rivera brothers left to hang out with old friends at the pool hall in town, while Nelly shopped at the traveling market that passed through La Perlita on Thursdays.

She strolled up and down between the two long rows of vendors displaying their varied household items that she couldn't find in the village's corner stores. She inspected the strawberries and blackberries for freshness, squeezed a few avocados and mangos for ripeness, and haggled over prices for the items she chose to purchase.

Among other things, she bought towels, plates, glasses, silverware, a candle, and a picture of *La Virgin de Guadalupe*, the patron saint of Mexico.

Returning home on the Barrio bus with her arms full, Nelly hung the large colorful picture on the living room wall, admiring the angel and moon at La Virgin's feet and the rays of sunlight that encircled her.

Lighting a candle, she knelt to pray. "Hail Mary, full of grace, the Lord is with thee. Blessed art thou among women and blessed is the fruit of thy womb, Jesús. Holy Mary, Mother of God, pray for me, a sinner. I know I have sinned against God. I am living with a man who is not my rightful husband and I am carrying his child. Please forgive me. I seek to do right by you, Virgin Maria, and your precious son, Jesús."

Tears filled Nelly's eyes. "Glory be to the Father, and to the Son, and to the Holy Spirit. As it was in the beginning, is now, and ever shall be, world without end. Amen."

"Okay, Mr. Rabbit," Nelly said, after her prayers. "It's time to face my mother. And I want to see her before my father gets home. Wish me luck."

Ten minutes later, Nelly stood at the front door of what had been her home for fourteen years. She noticed a giant poinsettia hanging by the front door and touched one of its red leaves. She felt like a stranger. Taking a deep breath to quiet her anxiety, she knocked.

Veronica, her three-year-old sister, opened the door. "Mamá," she squealed. "It's Nelly!"

Lidia rushed to the door, took Nelly into her arms and pulled her into the house. "Welcome home, Hija," she said, beaming.

"Thank you, Mamá."

"Veronica, go next door and tell Lupita to hurry home. Nelly has returned."

Warmth replaced Nelly's anxiety as she embraced her older sister, Lupita, a few minutes later. She felt the love of family and let her pent-up tears flow.

"You'll be living here again?" Veronica asked.

Nelly wiped her eyes with the back of her hand. "No, sweetie. Toro and I have a small place on the other side of the sports field."

"I missed you," Veronica said, climbing onto Nelly's lap.

Nelly kissed her little sister's forehead. "I have more news," she said.

"What's that?" her mother asked, walking towards the kitchen to prepare the evening meal.

"You're going to be an *abuela*. I'm pregnant."

Lupita and Veronica screamed with excitement and within seconds, Nelly felt her mother's loving arms wrap around her.

"Mamá, will you tell Papá for me...please?"

"I will. He'll be fine. You'll see. When will you and Toro marry?"

"That's up to Toro, Mamá."

⛊

Nelly's new life as Toro's partner, a soon-to-be mother, and caregiver to Toro's brothers began. She filled her days cleaning, preparing meals, shopping, and visiting her mother in the afternoons. Now a woman with a house full of hungry young men, Nelly learned from her Mamá how to grill iguana with fried plantains, make *pozolé*—hominy soup—and how to prepare a variety of seafood dishes.

Although excited to be back in La Perlita and close to her family, Nelly constantly worried about the changes she witnessed in Toro.

"Where were you all night?" she asked Toro one morning, two weeks after their arrival in La Perlita. "You left with Esteben after dinner and didn't get home until really late."

"I was working."

"What do you mean working? Where?"

"I'm building the business. I told you what I was going to do when we got here, amorcita."

Nelly fidgeted with the dishtowel and then set it down by the sink. "Yes, I know. I guess I hoped you'd change your mind and go back into construction or fishing."

"That won't support us, Nelly."

"But, what are you doing? I don't understand."

Toro placed his coffee cup on the small kitchen table and sat back in his chair. "I'm making contacts, I brought some pot and cocaine with me from Michoacán and I'm selling it at the pool hall. I'm getting the word out around the bars and beaches that I have pure product to sell."

"And?"

"And, I'm finding lots of buyers. Esteben and I leave in the morning for Michoacán to see my supplier and get more drugs."

"So it's really happening?"

Toro stood and walked to Nelly. He pulled her into his arms and kissed her on the forehead. "Yes, it's really happening. And what a difference compared to the few pesos we sold our plants for up in Santana. It's a two hundred percent profit for us between what I buy the drugs for in Los Reyes and the price I get on the street here. It's great money, Nelly."

"Toro, please. You said you were just going to sell 'some' drugs to make ends meet. This sounds different, like you're going to sell lots of drugs," she said, worry creeping into her voice.

"Don't worry, baby. I have this under control. I'm not going to become a big, dangerous drug lord like those mafia-types in Michoacán. I'll keep this small. Promise."

Nelly watched Toro's face fill with excitement. "But, I can't ignore the potential to make money. Lots of money," he added.

He's so excited with the possibilities of riches. I need to bury my concerns and be happy—for him and for us.

∽

"Nelly, look at this!" Toro said a few weeks later, removing a wad of five-hundred-peso bills out of his pocket and stacking them on the bed. "When I first started working for Don Joaquin in construction, it took me a whole week to earn one of these bills."

His face lit up with emotion. "Look," he said, counting out the bills. "There's twenty of them. It used to take me four months of working five and a half days a week to make this much!"

"Where did this money come from Toro?"

"Why are you frowning, woman?" Toro said, upset that the love of his life didn't look as excited as he felt.

"I'm just asking where so much money came from."

"This is a weekend worth of drug sales. We've been back in La Perlita for only two months and I can't keep up with the demand."

Toro placed the money between the slats of wood under their mattress. "Gerardo, my supplier in Michoacán hooked me up with a guy in Puerto Vallarta. I'm still working for Gerardo, but I don't have to go so far to replenish my supply anymore."

"Selling drugs is illegal, Toro. What if somebody turns you in as a dealer?"

"Don't worry. One of my old friends from here in the Barrio is a policeman. We talked. Those guys only make three-thousand pesos a month. That's a bit more than I made in construction. He's willing to help me out for a price. And he'll find me a couple of more of his buddies who will turn a blind eye as well. I'll have them on the payroll and we'll be fine."

Nelly turned her back on him and walked out of the room.

"Why aren't you excited?" Toro yelled as she left. "I'm doing this for us. For our family. For the baby!"

Frustration consuming him, Toro stormed out of the house and through the coconut groves, following his old trail down to the lagoon. Sitting on the bank he stared out into the water and watched egrets take flight. *It's only been a year. A year since I left La Perlita to go save my mom. So much has changed. It's not just me anymore. I have Nelly and a baby on the way. My brothers depend on me. I can't fail any of them.*

Toro inhaled deeply several times and exhaled, willing the pent up stress to leave his body. *I'm only seventeen—yet there are so many decisions to be made. I hate that Nelly doesn't agree with my selling drugs...but it's good money. Easy money. How can I not do this?*

⋰

Three months later, Toro bought a three-bedroom house with a large backyard. Nelly supervised her mother and sisters in packing up their small, concrete-floor rental.

"You and Toro are living a dangerous life, Hija," Lidia told her daughter as they packed up the house. "People are going to figure out, if they haven't already, that something illegal is happening—given all these luxuries."

"I know Mamá. It scares me too. I've told Toro the same thing, but he doesn't want to listen. He's confident that we live in a protected bubble."

⋰

"I like the brown floor tiles, Toro. They go perfect with the yellow and beige walls. And I love the kitchen with all the counter

80

space," Nelly said a few hours later. "This house feels warm and homey."

She held Toro's hand as he helped her maneuver her pregnant body from room to room in their new house.

Toro stopped to hug Nelly and patted her stomach. "This is the first major step for our family. And...I bought us a pit bull," he said. "Esteben will bring him home this afternoon. We'll call him Bullet. He'll protect you when I'm not around."

"Do we need protection, Toro?" she asked, concerned.

"We may. The more you have, the more you have to lose. It's better to be careful."

᷍

Over the next few days, Nelly watched Toro fill their home with new furniture and all the latest electronic gadgets as if money was no issue. At times, she wondered where the idealistic crusader-for-good Toro had gone.

He doesn't seem to notice the change, she thought as he drove up one afternoon with his friend, Alfonso, in a new white Ford F-250 truck.

"Why do we need this truck?" she asked, concerned about his spending.

"Good for business."

She recoiled against the irritation in his voice. "That's it? Good for business?"

"My territory is expanding. I need this to find new customers up and down the coast and to deliver drugs. I don't have time to use the bus anymore. And stop questioning me!"

"Hey man, I'm going to catch the bus back to Villa Caliente," Alfonso said. "Stop by later."

Toro grimaced as he looked at his old construction buddy and friend, Alfonso, who was now one of his main dealers. "Sure, sorry man. Obviously I didn't expect this reaction."

"I understand. My wife doesn't like what I'm doing either."

Nelly walked into the house and Toro followed. "Toro, what happened to keeping this small?"

"People want to *buy*, Nelly. Somebody is going to sell to them. So, I'm thinking...why not me? I'm not *forcing* anybody to use or buy drugs. I'm not the bad guy here."

Nelly shook her head and marched into the kitchen.

∽

The following month, June 2003, dark, heavy clouds hung in the air with a promise of rain. The rumble of distant thunder seemed to echo Nelly's inner turmoil. She knelt to pray—now praying for Toro's soul. She was watching his drinking increase along with his temper. *Lord, help me. He's becoming his father. When I mention it, he raises his hand as if he'll strike me. Just like his father.*

Days later, at age fifteen-and-a-half, Nelly gave birth to baby Felipe, who came into the world wailing at full-lung capacity.

A very proud Papa Toro held his infant son, looked into his large brown eyes, and kissed his wrinkled forehead. "I may be only seventeen, Hijo," he whispered. "But I promise to work hard and do all I can to give you the life I never had. You will want for nothing."

Toro was sure his baby heard him and understood.

ಏCHAPTER TWELVE≪

I s your mother coming over?" Toro asked, as they returned home from the hospital. He guided Nelly into the house, helped her into bed, and gently placed baby Felipe next to her.

"*Sí*. Mamá and Lupita will come every day for the next forty days during my confinement." Nelly placed a pillow behind her back and gathered her son close. "They'll take care of me and the house and do the cooking—like your aunt and I did for your mom."

"Okay, that's good, then. The boys and I'll be out most of the day. We have orders to deliver. I love you, Nelly."

"I love you, too, Toro." As he turned to leave, Nelly asked, "Toro, can we get married soon?"

Toro stopped in his tracks and looked at Nelly and their newborn son. "We're as good as married, amorcita. The rest is formality. Your parents never had an actual wedding, and neither did mine. A piece of paper won't change anything. I am your husband now. You are my wife. It's settled."

"I want us to be married—really married. I don't want to be the Samaritan woman at the well."

Toro sat down on the bed next to her. "What are you talking about? You don't want to be *what*?"

"The woman at the well in Samaria that the Bible talks about. She was living with a man who wasn't her husband, and Jesus called her on it."

Frustrated, Toro got up and walked to the door. "This is 2003, not biblical times. I'm not worried about something from so far in the past. Jesus Christ has more important things to do than judge us. Adios. I have work to do."

Nelly's face fell, and tears came to her eyes. She wrapped her arms around baby Felipe, who lay snuggled in a soft blue blanket, looking like a tiny burrito. She caressed his light brown cheeks. *Someday, Hijo. Someday we'll be a real family.*

⋘

Two months after Felipe's birth, Toro announced at breakfast, "I'm going up to Michoacán."

"Why? What's up?" Esteben asked, finishing his coffee.

"I want to go with you," Miguel said. "I'm bored."

"What does a twelve-year-old have to be bored about?" Toro said, raising his voice. "Obviously your life is too easy. At twelve, I was working in the hot sun, fishing, to help feed our family."

"I'm out of school for the summer. And I'm bored," Miguel said, his hazel green eyes lit with rebellion.

"Calm down, Toro," Julio said. "He's just being honest. While we're out partying and making connections, he's here with Nelly and the baby. Of course he's bored."

"Well, he's too young to be out running around with us in the middle of the night."

"I'm tired of being treated like a baby!" Miguel shouted.

Toro stopped a moment and looked at Miguel. *He looks a lot like our grandfather with those hazel green eyes. I must admit he's growing up. He's already three inches taller than Esteben. But I'm not taking him to Michoacán. It's bad enough I'm putting Esteben at risk.*

"So, you didn't answer my question, Toro. What's going on that we need to make that trip?" Esteben asked.

Toro refocused his attention. "There's a problem. Papá called me earlier this morning. Our supplier, Gerardo was killed a couple of days ago."

"What?" Nelly said, from the bedroom. "Killed how?"

"He apparently was shot by a *sicario*."

"An assassin?" Carrying the baby in her arms, Nelly returned to the kitchen and sat down at the table. "Why do you have to go where people are being murdered? That's crazy."

Toro's patience snapped. "I'll do what I have to do. Don't question me!"

"I have a right to be concerned, Toro. It's too dangerous."

Toro bolted from the table. "You have no right to tell me what to do, woman!"

"Whoa, Bro," Esteben interjected. "She's just worried."

Toro grabbed a beer from the refrigerator and stormed out the door. They heard him roaring off in his truck, spinning gravel under the tires.

The brothers sat quietly looking at each other.

Nelly cradled Felipe and let the tears flow, unhindered, down her cheeks.

"He's getting more and more like our dad," Julio said. "That's not good."

Esteben stood up. "He's under a lot of stress. The tourists are gone and won't be back until November. That's a huge hit on our income."

"Well, he doesn't need to yell at me!" Miguel said.

That evening, Toro left Miguel and Julio at home with Nelly while he and Esteben set out for the eight hour drive into the Santana hills.

"Toro, what's eating at you?" Esteben asked, an hour into their journey. "You've changed."

"Of course I've changed. I'm a husband, a father, and we have money for luxuries now."

"Not the money, Bro. I mean *you* have changed. You're short-tempered and you're drinking day and night. This isn't like you."

Toro kept his eyes ahead on the road.

Esteben waited.

"I didn't want this life, ever," he finally said. "But doors opened. I had choices, and I took the door with opportunity to climb out of poverty and give my family a good life."

"And?" Esteben asked.

"And with this choice comes risks. Like Nelly not approving. I feel the distance between us. Like she has stopped respecting me, man."

Toro fought to regain his composure and keep a lid on his emotions. "And the more into this drug world I get the riskier it gets. Like some low-life assassins killing Gerardo. The guy has a wife and three kids! What did he do to deserve that?"

Toro rolled down the driver's side window and breathed in the cool air. "The more responsibility I take on, like expanding the selling area, the more danger I'm in. I can't deny that my involvement in the drug world puts Nelly and Felipe and you...everybody at risk."

"Have you thought about just getting out? We've only been doing this for eight months. We can get out before it's too late."

"No. I owe too much. I owe on this truck, on the new house. I can't support all of us on seventy damn dollars a week working in construction. When Papá pulled me out of school, he ended my chances of having a profession—of having an honorable way to support a wife and family."

"You've just turned eighteen, Toro. I'm sixteen and Julio is fourteen. Between the three of us we could do something. Start some type of business. Pull together and earn money that doesn't bring such risks."

"Like what? You two have ninth grade educations. I only went to part of fifth. What are we going to do that will give us homes and vehicles and stacks of money under the mattress?"

The two brothers sat in silence. Neither had an answer.

⌁

"Good morning, Mamá," Toro said, opening the front door of his parent's home at dawn. "You're up early. Did Papá tell you we were coming today?"

"Yes, he did. It's so good to see you," she said, hugging her two oldest sons. "It's been over eight months. Here, sit down for some coffee and rolls, and then go take a nap for a few hours. You must be exhausted."

"Nah, we're okay. We took turns driving and sleeping. Coffee will help though. Make it strong," Toro said, happy to be home, but hating the reason for the visit.

"Is Papá awake?" Esteben asked.

"I heard the shower a few minutes ago. He'll be out soon. And your uncle will be over for coffee in a few minutes.

ॐ

"So, what's going on?" Toro asked his father a while later. "You sounded really worried on the phone yesterday."

"Things are heating up," Enrique said, sitting down at the table. "The assassinations of Gerardo and several other suppliers is just the start."

"What's changing?" Esteben asked.

"Several things. A couple of months ago the military arrested the leader of the Valencia family cartel."

"Yes, I heard about that." Toro finished his coffee and buttered his roll.

"That arrest weakened them," Enrique said. "For protection, the new Valencia leader agreed to associate with the Sinaloa cartel under 'El Chapo' Guzman. The Valencias are now a branch of what they call the Sinaloa Federation."

"That's not good," Toro said.

Just then his Uncle Juan opened the kitchen door and joined them. Toro and Esteben rose to greet their uncle with quick shoulder hugs and handshakes.

"Good morning, Juan," Maria said, entering the kitchen with Jesus Antonio in her arms. "There's hot coffee and sweet rolls."

"That sounds great. Thanks. Sorry to bother you so early."

"You're not. I was up early waiting for these two to arrive." Maria looked fondly at her sons. "And I've got to wake Ricky soon to get him off to school.

Toro reached out his arms for his youngest brother, hugged him and placed sixteen-month-old Jesus on his lap. "He looks like me," he said, smiling.

"No. He doesn't have your round face," Esteben countered. "His is more angular, like mine. He's a spitting image of me. Pass him over here."

Jesus Antonio began to cry and Maria lifted him out of Esteben's arms. "Okay you two, give him to me. He doesn't remember either of you. You'll have to stay here a while so he gets to know you."

As Maria left the room, Juan picked up the conversation. "What's happening is not good at all, boys. You can expect bullets to fly and a lot more deaths."

"So what happened to Gerardo, Tio? Who killed him and why?" Toro asked, still unable to believe the news.

"Word on the street? He and others were eliminated as part of this turf war. Gerardo worked with La Familia. The Valencias want this part of Michoacán back under their control. They're sending out the message that you either work with them or they'll kill you."

Esteben fidgeted in his chair. "Obviously that means La Familia still hasn't pushed out the Valencia cartel as you'd hoped. Are you two concerned? Aren't you associated with La Familia?"

Toro watched his younger brother's uneasiness. *I'm sure he'd much rather be in La Perlita, kicking a soccer ball with his friends or drinking with cute girls in bikinis on the beach than hearing this stuff.*

"You just pay for their protection. Right?" Toro clarified. "And what are they going to do about these deaths? Retaliate?"

"Yes and yes," Enrique replied. "We don't work directly for them, and yes, we expect them to retaliate—big time. A huge cartel war is brewing. I predict fighting and killing will break out all over Mexico. Several groups are pushing for control of Michoacán."

Esteben shook his head in confusion. "But why this continued fight over Michoacán? We're not even near the U.S. border where the major drug smuggling happens."

Juan poured himself more coffee. "As we explained to Toro some months ago, the Valencias have been working with the Colombians and smuggling cocaine shipments from South and Central America for years. Part of that smuggling route is right through Michoacán to the ports of Lazaro Cardenas and Manzanillo. From there they smuggle shiploads into the United States.

Esteben nodded. "Oh. Okay, I get it."

"Do you boys realize what the markup for cocaine is?" Enrique asked. "I read a drug enforcement report in the paper last week. The traffickers pay two thousand dollars for a kilo of cocaine here in Mexico. That is leaf to lab. That same kilo sells for up to a hundred thousand dollars in the U.S."

Toro looked at his father in disbelief.

"How is that possible?" Esteben asked

"It's resold and cut along the way. By the time it's pushed in rich gringo neighborhoods up north, it's sold for a hundred dollars a gram. With a thousand grams in a kilo...well, you went through middle school, Esteben. Do the math."

"I get the incentive for controlling the transportation routes, Papá," Toro said. "The cartels are making more money than oil producers. I don't want any part of that."

"President Fox says he wants the traffickers arrested, and the cartels extinguished," Juan added. "But I can't see how he's going to accomplish that. There's too much corruption throughout the police departments and the government." Juan stood up and stretched. "I have a bad feeling about this, boys. I think Mexico is in for a huge cartel war, worse than the old mafia wars shown in those Godfather movies."

"Can't we just stay out of it?" Esteben asked. "All we want to do is keep beach tourists happy with a bit of coke and weed."

"I can't stay out of it, Hermano. I need a new supplier. So, Tio— do I stay with La Familia or go with the Valencia's Sinaloa cartel? Which one will be on top next month?" Toro asked.

"Only God knows," his uncle said. "Roll the dice."

❧CHAPTER THIRTEEN❦

Three years later, July 21, 2006

H appy birthday, amor," Nelly whispered to Toro.

Toro opened his bloodshot eyes, feeling the pain threatening to split open his skull. He glared at Nelly's smiling face and turned to face the wall. "It's too early. Shut the curtains and the door."

"It's your twenty-first birthday. Felipe made a gift for you."

"Later! Let me sleep."

"It's already ten o'clock. Your son has been waiting to see you."

"*Luego.* Now, get out!"

Nelly walked back to the living room and gathered three-year-old Felipe into her arms. "It's okay, Son. Papá will be up later, and you can show him your drawing. Now, go outside and play. Be quiet so your daddy doesn't get mad. He's resting for his party tonight."

Nelly's heart broke as she lifted Jessica, her five-month-old daughter, out of the crib and watched her son's sweet face fall in disappointment.

❦

Two hours later, Toro attempted to get out of bed, but fell back onto his pillow. With eyes closed, he reached for the aspirin bottle by the side of the bed. After succeeding in popping off the top of the bottle, he swallowed four pills with a sip of water. *I hate these hangovers!*

He spent a few moments regretting his drinking; something he knew made Nelly angry. But he couldn't stop. He liked the way he felt when drunk. Like he was king of the world with no cares whatsoever.

Nelly doesn't know what I've had to do to keep others from taking over my territory. I don't want her to know I've ordered their 'disappearance' when they wouldn't stop selling. I gave them chances to leave. They didn't. This is big business. It is them or me. What's done is done. I sent out a message I won't be messed with.

He thought back on how his weed and cocaine business had flourished over the years and how the profits abounded. *I'm not a bad person. I'm a businessman and I do give back.*

He had used his wealth to sponsor La Perlita soccer teams and employ workers to build him houses. He helped the local economy through his spending on construction materials, furniture and electronics. He hosted large, extravagant parties at home or in local restaurants and even gave money for the mayor to buy Christmas presents for all the children in town.

But his father had been right. The drug war between cartels and between the federal police and cartels had begun escalating under Vicente Fox's presidency.

As he waited for the aspirin to take effect, Toro stretched his arms up over his head. He thought back to a conversation he'd had with Esteben a year earlier on a drive into Puerto Vallarta to pick up product.

"This escalating violence doesn't surprise me," he'd told his brother. "This is the first time we've ever seen so much money within our reach. Real money has always been for the corporate heads and the politicians. We never had a chance of making a good life for ourselves until smart Mexicans took over the drug trafficking from the Colombians."

"I get it too, Bro," Esteben had responded. "I don't like it though. Thousands of Mexicans are killing each other to get rich."

I can't believe I'm now one of 'them', Toro thought. *Willing to kill to keep big money coming in. Where did the old Toro go?*

∾

After a half hour, Toro felt his headache lessen. He tried rising again. Perched on the side of the bed, head in hands waiting for a wave of nausea to pass, he took inventory of his life. *Twenty-one. Twenty-one and powerful. He liked the feeling. Profits are good. People respect me. Those who fear me have a reason to.*

I shouldn't have waited so long to start selling the meth. Cheap and addictive. Lots of repeat customers.

Toro succeeded in standing upright and stretched. *And now that I'm loaning money at a stiff interest rate, I'll have income even when the tourists are gone.* He walked into the bathroom and looked at himself in the mirror. *Powerful and indestructible.*

∾

To celebrate Toro's twenty-first birthday, Nelly had invited two hundred people to an extravagant gala on the street outside their house. She hired a clown to entertain the children, and a live band to regale their guests into the wee hours of the morning.

Enrique and Maria arrived with Toro's two youngest siblings a few hours before the celebration, and Uncle Juan and his family drove in right behind them.

"Welcome, Mamá," Toro said, bending down to give his mother a bear hug. He shook hands with his father and uncle and embraced his aunt. *"Bienvenidos."*

Jesús Antonio, now four years old, jumped from the back of the pickup truck followed by twelve-year-old Ricky.

"Felipe!" Jesus Antonio squealed.

Felipe's face lit up with joy. "'sus!"

With a smile, Toro watched the two little boys run off to play. Pride expanded his chest.

⌁

At eight o'clock, Nelly wiped the perspiration from her brow and put lids on the four large pots of *pozole*. "Do you think we'll have enough food?" she asked.

Her mother, Lidia, looked around the kitchen. "We have enough pozole, birria, pinto beans, salads, rice, and fresh tortillas to feed an army."

"I agree," her mother-in-law said. "You're more than ready."

Esteben opened the front door and entered with four cases of Corona. "Julio and I parked our trucks at both ends of the block. They'll be no through traffic tonight." He set the cases down in the kitchen. "We have ten ice chests full of Corona and Tecate outside. We'll leave the extra beer in here."

Julio followed Esteben in, carrying the cases of Tecate. "The tables and chairs are all set up. There are bottles of tequila, limes, and big bottles of Coca Cola at each table."

"I think we're pretty much ready, then," Nelly said, relieved. She thanked her mother, sisters, and mother-in-law for their help and walked down the hallway and into her bedroom to dress for the party.

A few moments later, Nelly sat on the bed holding Jessica and watching Toro shave. "Please don't drink too much tonight, *amor*. I don't want the night to be spoiled, and you've barely recuperated from last night's binge."

"Don't start with me. This is my night, my party, and I'll damn well do what I want. I'm the man of this house and don't you forget it!"

Nineteen-year-old Nelly took a deep breath and willed herself to stay calm. She'd learned to acquiesce under Toro's quick fits of anger. *I won't ruin this night. I can't ruin tonight with another fight.*

She knew life felt good to Toro. It had taken a while, but she knew he had succeeded in ridding himself of any feelings of guilt for his actions—drinking away all semblance of a conscience. She'd heard the rumors about people "going missing" because of her husband. She didn't want to believe her Toro was capable of killing a human being. *But is he capable of ordering it?* she asked herself. *How far would he go to keep his sellers in line and his territory intact?*

Walking out of the bedroom, Nelly let out a deep breath to steady her nerves. She handed baby Jessica to her mother and dialed a friend to make sure the mariachis were on schedule to sing the *Las Mañanitas* traditional birthday song for Toro right at midnight. *For better or worse, let the party begin.*

∽

Toro greeted his guests as they started arriving at ten o'clock. Drink in hand, he accepted their congratulations with a smile. Gifts started filling the gift table while Nelly and her sisters piled plates with hot food and his brothers offered their guests cold drinks.

"The clown is here!" Felipe and Jesús screamed in unison a few minutes later, clapping their hands. The children gathered in a large group as the lively music and games began.

"Nice turnout," Esteben said later, handing Toro a cold Corona. "Some of the guests want *mota*. You want us to sell it or give it away?"

"Give it away. Makes for good business. We'll get it back later in increased sales."

"Sounds good. By the way, the musicians have arrived from Autlan. They're set up and ready to play."

As if on cue, fireworks exploded into the night, three trumpets sounded and the ten-piece band started their first song.

Toro, his family, and friends partied into the early hours of the morning.

∽

The following afternoon, finally sober enough to get out of bed; Toro joined his father and uncle for lunch before they headed home.

"That was quite a party you threw last night, Son," Enrique said. His eyes were bloodshot, but he had a smile on his face.

"Well, Papá, when you're entertaining and feeding over two hundred of your closest friends, who either buy drugs from you or owe you money, you're bound to have a good time."

"You sound a bit cynical, Sobrino," Juan said. "But happy birthday anyway. Let's drink to the next twenty-one. *Salud.*"

Enrique lifted his bottle of Tecate. "Salud."

"Salud," Toro echoed.

"Cheers!" Esteben added, sitting down at the table.

"What's the news up in Michoacán?" Toro asked, as Nelly served them left-over pozole. "My new supplier doesn't say much."

"It's best that way," his father said. "The players change from day to day, cartel to cartel, and you don't know who to trust."

Juan motioned for his wife to bring them more tortillas. "I'm sure you've heard that the Zetas have a presence in Michoacán now."

"What? Los Zetas? Why? They're psychopaths!" Esteben said, shocked by the news.

Juan dipped a tortilla into his soup and looked at his nephews. "That they are. They're ex-military, heavily armed, and deadly. I think La Familia is desperate. They've been trying to get rid of the Valencias for years. Now they're counting on Los Zetas to kill or chase them out."

Esteben stared. "This doesn't sound good."

Toro stopped eating. "I thought the Zetas were the mortal enemies of La Familia."

"That's what I'm saying," Juan said. "They *were* enemies. Now they're allies. You just don't know who to trust."

"You got your plaza from the La Familia, right?" Enrique asked his son.

"Yes. Back when they went from being a mere vigilante group to drug traffickers. My selling area is from here and up the coast to Punta Arena. My supply of drugs comes from one of their lieutenants stationed near Puerto Vallarta. I place and manage dealers in this area. For example, you met Alfonso last night. He's in charge of the drug sales in Villa Caliente. He works for me."

"Be careful, Sobrino," Juan said. "Los Zetas are the ones organizing the plazas now, and they're executing anyone who even talks to a rival cartel."

"And those executions aren't pretty," Enrique added. "Something big is going to happen. I can just feel it."

"You've been saying that for years, Papá," Toro said. "Stop worrying."

Preparing for bed that evening, Toro thought back to the conversation with his father and uncle. Foreboding engulfed him. He remembered his earlier inventory—*powerful and indestructible. Am I?*

✍

Two months later, in September, Nelly rushed into the bedroom, and shook Toro. "Wake up. Wake up!"

"*Estás loca? Que pasa?*"

"Come see what's on the news. Something happened in Michoacán. Hurry." She ran back into the hall. "Esteben, chicos, wake up!"

Toro, Esteben, Julio, and Miguel stumbled into the living room from different directions.

Gathered around the large flat-screen television, the small group watched the news coverage.

"Last year, there were fifteen hundred murders here in Mexico related to drug trafficking," the reporter said, showing a graph set up next to him. "That number is up to two thousand so far this year."

"So what?" Toro said, losing interest. "Things like that happen around the big cities and border towns."

"Shhh, listen," Esteben said.

"La Familia gunmen fired shots into the ceiling of the *Sol y Sombra* nightclub last night in Uruapan, Michoacán," the grim-faced reporter said. "Witnesses say they gave orders to the patrons to lie down on the floor."

Nelly gasped as a gruesome photograph came on the screen. "The gunmen then threw five human heads wrapped in plastic onto the dance floor."

"Oh my God, oh my God, oh my God." Nelly took rosary beads from her pocket and started fingering them, one by one.

Toro kept his eyes glued to the television.

The commentator continued, "The gunmen left the following note praising their deed—'The Family doesn't kill for money; it doesn't kill women; it doesn't kill innocent people—only those who deserve to die. Everyone should know...this is divine justice.'"

"What does this mean, Toro?" Nelly wiped tears from her eyes with shaking hands. "Are we safe? I'm scared."

"We're okay, aren't we, Hermano?" Julio asked.

Toro grabbed his cell phone from the bedroom. "Hold on, hold on. Let me find out."

Moments later, his father answered his call. "Papá, have you seen the news?"

"Yes, Son. I'm here in Santana at a coffee shop, and we're all watching it," Enrique responded, concern in his voice.

Toro motioned for his brothers to gather near and put his cell on speaker phone. "What happened? What's this about?"

"It looks like that was the official announcement of La Familia Michoacana's rise to power. Toro, this is what we were telling you at your birthday party. This show of public gruesome force is just the beginning."

Esteben raised his voice. "The beginning of *what*?"

"Of La Familia rising in numbers, strength, and brutality, Hijo—of all-out war to rid the entire state of Michoacán of all criminals, cartels, and crystal meth. It's what La Familia has been promising for years."

Toro looked at Nelly and his brothers sitting together on the couch and for a quick second wondered how he'd gotten them to this dangerous point—all he'd wanted to do was give them a good life. "But Papá, why the brutality?"

"Hold on, Son. Your Uncle Juan wants to talk to you."

Toro motioned for Nelly to bring him a beer. *What have I got us messed up in?*

"Toro," Juan said, "those heads they rolled into that disco last night? They say those five guys were some petty criminals who raped a young girl a couple of days ago. La Familia doesn't trust the police or the government to protect us. They're taking over."

Toro felt lead flow through his body and sat back in his chair. "So, what does that mean for us? For you? For Michoacán?"

"I think it means retaliation and more deaths," Juan said. "La Familia used Los Zetas to get the Valencias out. Now they've aligned with the Sinaloa cartel to go against Los Zetas. Like we said at your party, nobody knows who to trust, who to pay, who to support."

Eight weeks later, Toro opened the newspaper at a local taco stand and found a full-page manifesto written by La Familia Michoacana. "Listen to this, Esteben. La Familia is publicizing their mission. This says they're going to *'Eradicate from the state of Michoacán kidnapping, extortion in person and by telephone, paid assassinations, express kidnapping, tractor-trailer and auto theft, home robberies done by people like those mentioned—those who have made the state of Michoacán an unsafe place.'*

"I'm sure they're talking about the Valencias." Toro said. "They go on to say *'Our sole motive is that we love our state and are no longer willing to see our people's dignity trampled on.'*"

"This is a good thing, then," Esteben said. "We're not trampling on anybody's dignity. And we're not selling in Michoacán."

"Are you looking for a silver lining in a very dark cloud, Esteben?" Toro asked, jokingly to hide his own concern.

After placing three bottles of cold beer on the table, Julio pulled up a chair. "What are you reading, Bro?"

"It's a statement from La Familia," Toro replied. "Listen to this, *'...there are people who do not understand us, but we know that, in the areas most affected, they understand our actions, since now it is possible to ward off these delinquents who come from other states and whom we will not allow to enter Michoacán and continue committing crimes. We are eradicating completely from the state the retail sale of the lethal drug known as ice, as it is one of the worst drugs, one that causes irreversible damage to society.'"*

Toro stopped reading and downed half the bottle of beer. "They've been saying that for a while. They don't want crystal meth sold within the state of Michoacán, but I know for a fact they produce it and export it. My supplier gets it from somebody up the line who works for La Familia."

Esteben flashed his impish smile at their waitress. She placed three large plates of beef tacos on the table.

"Gracias, Lucia," he said. "By the way, could I have your phone number?"

Toro and Julio smiled as pretty, long-haired Lucia wrote her number on a napkin and placed it into Esteben's shirt pocket. "Don't lose it," she said and sashayed away.

Esteben's eyes followed her. "She's so cute and petite," he said. "Just my size."

"Hey Bro, you robbing the cradle?" Julio teased. "She can't be more than ten."

"Nah...I'm good. She's fifteen. I'm nineteen," he said, sitting up straight. "I've been watching her around town for months and danced with her at a party a couple of weeks ago. She's hot, and I think she's into me."

After teasing Esteben about the follies of falling in love, the brothers finished their meal, and Julio returned to the newspaper article. "I'm thinking about what La Familia manifesto says. It's hypocritical, isn't it?" he said. "They say they're getting rid of crystal meth and yet they make the stuff?"

Toro threw his napkin on his empty plate and sat back in his chair. "The way they run their organization is definitely unusual. By exporting meth they're making tons of money to fund their cause, while saving their own people," he explained. "And I've heard that if a member of La Familia uses any drug—they're punished and sent to reform camps."

"I actually agree with that part," Julio said. "You can't run a business if you're jacked up." Picking up the paper, he scanned the manifesto. "This part sounds like they're talking about those severed heads they threw into the disco a couple of months ago, *'Unfortunately, to eradicate the ills we have mentioned, we have had to resort to robust strategies, as we have seen that this is the only way to bring order to the state. We will not allow it to get out of control again.'"*

Finishing the article, Julio laid the paper on the table. "Simply put, they've marked their territory and won't allow people from other states to commit crimes in Michoacán."

Esteben signaled Lucia to bring him another beer. "They're serious, but we're good, right? We're not selling anything in Michoacán."

"I need to talk to our supplier," Toro replied, crossing his arms and trying to hide any semblance of fear. "Some of their message doesn't make sense. They want to set a moral compass. Yet, they're distributing drugs. But they'll kill others who are doing the same thing. We're working for them—even though we're pretty far down the line of importance. They should protect us, not send someone after us...I think."

❧CHAPTER FOURTEEN❧

February 2008

Toro and his brothers watched the drug war escalate just as their father had been predicting for years. La Familia had rid Michoacán of the Valencias by working with Los Zetas. And then, aligning themselves with Chapo Guzman's Sinaloa cartel, they successfully rid Michoacán of Los Zetas. Seeing the billions of potential dollars in drug growing and trafficking, they left behind their "vigilante" status and expanded drug trafficking along the U.S. - Mexico border. Without direct access to the border, La Familia paid tariffs to other organized crime groups controlling the border corridors.

Toro felt safe after having stayed loyal to the La Familia during the conflict. From the safety of La Perlita fishing village, he watched La Familia cartel corrupt government officials in both Michoacán and the state of Jalisco—providing employment through the drug trade and essentially fulfilling the police's role in resolving domestic disputes. He used that methodology in La Perlita and did not fear the local police.

❧

"Please, Toro," Nelly implored one Sunday in early February. "Come to Mass with the kids and me this morning and talk with Father Cesar."

"Stop hounding me, Nelly," he shouted. "What good can talking to the priest do me?"

"He can pray for you. He can protect your soul. You used to believe in God, in Jesus, in good things."

"I'm beyond that now, Nelly. No talking to the 'Man of God' will save me. I'm entrenched in this life more than you know. It's been over six years. I can't get out, even if I wanted to—and I don't."

❧

Days later, Toro held Jessica, who had just celebrated her second birthday on Valentine's Day. Scowling, he flipped through the pages of his ever-present notebook. The worn pages bore proof of money lent and money owed as well as drugs purchased on credit.

Jessica, apparently mesmerized by the turning pages, reached out and grabbed the notebook, snatching it from her father's hands.

"Jessica, stop! Nelly, come get this child. I can't work with her grabbing everything."

"Toro, I'm busy. Be nice."

"I am nice. Come get her."

Bright-eyed Jessica with her curly, raven-black hair looked like the spitting image of Nelly. She smiled as her mother lifted her off Toro's lap and placed her on the floor. "Come on, sweetie," she said, leading Jessica to her bedroom.

Toro's gaze followed his wife and daughter as they walked away, appreciating their beauty for just a moment. Turning back to his account book, he peered down the rows of more than a hundred names, followed by numbers and percentages: Julio Luis, $1,000 pesos, 5% interest, $50 pesos due each Friday. Eladio Sanchez, $5,000 pesos; 10% interest, $500 pesos due each Friday. Juana Lopez, $800 pesos, 15% interest, $120 pesos due each Saturday. On and on the names went.

Nelly peered through the bedroom door at Toro, hunched over his book, pencil in hand. "How do you decide what interest rate to charge?" she asked.

"Depends on how much I like the person, and how much I think they can pay."

"I saw my parents name in there," she said. "They came to you for money?"

"Your mom. She wanted extra spending money. I'm not charging her interest, though."

"She borrowed a lot. I hope she pays you back," Nelly said, concern in her voice. "She doesn't make much money selling her tamales."

"She put her house up as collateral. I think she'll pay."

Suddenly, Felipe burst through the front door. "Mamá, where's my soccer ball?" he yelled as he ran into his room.

"Wherever you left it, Hijo."

"Mamá! My soccer ball. Where is it?"

"Look out back," Nelly said, frustrated.

Nelly's younger brother, Daniel, came through the front door as Felipe scrambled out the back. "Hey, Toro."

"Hey, Daniel."

"Can Felipe come with me to the sports field to kick the soccer ball around?"

"You're going to watch out for him? He's not even five," Toro said.

"I will. I promise. I'm going to be nine this year, you know."

Toro thought a moment, tapping his pencil on the table. "No, I don't like it. Take Miguel with you, or don't go."

Just then, Miguel walked into the kitchen from the back yard, soccer ball and Felipe in hand. "I heard that. I'll go. It's better than cleaning out the goat pen. Come on, boys."

"Be back in an hour," Nelly yelled. "And Miguel, watch Felipe, not the girls. You have too many girlfriends already."

"How can any hot-blooded Mexican have too many *novias*, Nelly?" he said, flashing his broad smile, showing off his dimples.

Toro watched them hurry out of the house. *It's been so long since I've kicked a soccer ball*, he thought.

"Nelly, let's take the kids to the beach Sunday. My brothers can go with us. See if your mom will let us take Veronica, Daniel...and Ruben's kids."

Nelly counted on her fingers. "That's fifteen counting your brother's girlfriends. You sure?"

Toro laughed. "Let's do it. Fill the truck with food, drinks, and family."

Nelly smiled.

❦

At a secluded part of La Perlita's beach days later, Toro quieted his racing mind. He watched Felipe chase his cousins in and out of the waves. Jessica built sand castles with her aunt Veronica, while Nelly sunbathed on a blanket, chatting with Esteben's girlfriend, Lucia.

At almost twenty-three years of age, Toro prided himself on having created a family and an abundant life, wanting for nothing.

Esteben, at age twenty, worked as his second-in-command. He and Lucia, along with their baby girl, lived with him and Nelly as they saved money for their future. Eighteen-year-old Julio had moved in with his girlfriend's family. He was building a house in La Perlita and had recently bought a Chevy truck—his pride and joy.

Toro glanced over at Miguel playing soccer with Daniel. He'd graduated from middle school, ran errands for his brothers and was learning to fatten and sell goats. *It's good. We're good.*

After passing around bottles of cold beer and sodas, Esteben sat on a blanket next to Toro. "What a group we are," he said.

Toro smiled. "I was just thinking the same thing, Bro."

"We've come a long way since stepping off the bus from Michoacán six years ago," Esteben mused.

"Yeah. We arrived with nothing but a few pesos and those first bags of marijuana and some coke to sell. Now we have everything we want," Toro said, high-fiving his brother.

Esteben took a deep breath. "I've been thinking about increasing my savings and starting a small construction business someday...and leaving this life to you,"

"Really, little brother? You'd walk away from this?"

"I think so. Remember how you used to say the only way out of this life is in a box? Well I don't want that to be me. And Lucia really doesn't want me in this life."

Esteben and Toro remained silent for a moment, until Esteben asked, "Would you ever walk away, Toro?"

Toro didn't hesitate before answering. "No. For two reasons. I'm too entrenched and owe a huge debt to La Familia. And...I never want to be poor again."

"Then, what's next?" Esteben asked.

"We stay alive and in control of our plaza...that's what's next. You're right to be concerned. This narco world is crazy. So, we stay loyal to our bosses, keep the police happy, and protect our own. We need to buy more guns and ammunition, but we'll discuss that later. Today, let's play."

Jumping up off the sand, Toro ran toward his younger brothers, capturing the soccer ball meant for Miguel.

❧CHAPTER FIFTEEN❦

Lying in his hammock in mid-December, 2009, a sullen Toro took inventory. "I've amassed a small fortune. Sales are on the rise, I own half-a-dozen homes, a lucrative loan-shark business, goats to fatten and sell for a hefty profit, all the jewelry and material goods I could ever want, and an arsenal to protect us. So, why do I feel so....down?"

Maybe it's because Sandy is pregnant and I'm going to have to tell Nelly I have another woman...and a baby on the way.

Just as Toro set out to drown his concerns in alcohol, Esteben drove down the street in his new Toyota Pickup and parked in front of the house. "Hey, hermano. I got your text. What's up?" Esteben asked, shutting the truck door.

Even though Toro knew Nelly and the kids were in town at the Thursday street market, he still looked around to make sure they were alone. "Sandy's pregnant. She told me today. And not just a little pregnant—she's due in April. I've got to tell Nelly...before she finds out. It's not going to be a good thing."

"Oh, man. Fireworks are going to explode. Nelly isn't going to take this well, Toro."

"That's what I'm here thinkin'. But...what's she going to do? Leave me? Leave this life I've created for her? Where would she go?"

"I don't know, Bro, but I'm glad I'm not you right now. My Lucia would kill me if I showed up with that news."

Toro laid his massive frame back in the hammock and chugged a bottle of beer. "Yah...I figure I better hide those guns in the bedroom."

Esteben chuckled and sat down. Leaning back in his chair he settled in to spend some time with his big brother.

"You brought this on yourself you know. So, why'd you do it? Why did you hook up with Sandy?"

Toro thought about Esteben's question. "Maybe because Sandy is easy to be with. She never knew the 'other' me, so there's no judgment, no disappointment. She loves and accepts me for who I am right now."

A few moments later, Toro continued. "I love Nelly. I've always loved her...but it seems like everything I do is a disappointment. She makes me feel 'wrong'. It gets tiring."

"Wow, that's some deep thinking. I didn't know you had that in you, man," Esteben said, teasing his brother. "I know how to cheer you up, though."

"How? You have some good news?"

"Depends on what good news means. We're still alive and thriving. That's good," Esteben said and laughed.

"Anything else?" Toro asked, losing patience.

Esteben adjusted his black baseball cap. "OK, it's not good news, but it'll take your mind off your immediate troubles."

"Just tell me, man. I'm in no mood for small talk."

"I just read some statistics in the paper. Seven thousand people died last year in drug-related violence and it's up to nearly ten thousand this year, with two more weeks to go."

"That's not good," Toro said. He got out of the hammock to get another beer.

Esteben accepted a cold Corona from Toro when he returned from the house. "You know how the military killed the leader of Los Zetas a couple of weeks ago?"

"Yeah."

"Well, the head of the Beltran Leyva cartel was killed in a shootout with Mexican forces in Cuernavaca today."

"Two more idiots gone," Toro replied. "And a new leader will take over in a span of moments, anyway. I don't know much about the Leyva cartel, but the military can kill all those damn Zetas," Toro said coldly. He settled back into the hammock. "Both President's Fox and Calderon have tried to end drug cartels in Mexico, without success. But maybe Calderon's strategy is working. He's using that kingpin strategy the Colombian government used."

"What's that?" Esteben asked.

"The military works on the cartels' weaknesses. They intercept communications, screw with the supply and distribution of drugs, and seize assets. Once they weaken the group, they find and arrest the kingpin and the other top leaders, including the kingpin's potential successors."

"Okay, so that's why it's called the kingpin strategy. Are we at risk?"

"Nobody cares about us. But, about six months ago, the Attorney General labeled La Familia Michoacána the most violent criminal organization in Mexico. I'm sure Calderon wants to dismantle it. I think we're unknown, though."

"Why would La Familia be labeled the most violent? Los Zetas are, aren't they?" Esteben asked.

Straddling the hammock, Toro ran fingers through his messy hair. "I think it's because La Familia is launching brazen attacks against government forces. Calderon is on a retribution mission."

"Dang, here comes Nelly," Esteben warned.

The brothers watched her pull in behind Esteben's truck, park and begin handing Felipe and Jessica grocery bags from the back of the vehicle.

"I think I"ll get Lucia and the baby and head over to Julio's," Esteben said. "I definitely don't want to be in the mix when you enlighten Nelly as to your recent extra-curricular activities."

"Thanks for having my back," Toro said, his voice dripping sarcasm.

❧

Later that night, with the kids asleep and the house quiet, Toro approached Nelly as she finished cleaning the kitchen. "I have something to tell you," he said gently.

"What's that?" Nelly asked, turning from the sink to look at her husband.

"I know you're going to be angry."

Nelly laid the dish cloth on the sink and with dread in her heart said, "What did you do this time, Toro?"

Not finding any words to soften the blow, Toro swallowed his guilt and blurted it out. "I started hanging out with Sandy, and... well...she's pregnant."

Nelly stared as if trying to make sure she'd heard him right. "You did what? Which Sandy?"

"Sandy Lopez."

"That tramp?" shouted Nelly. "She's living with some gringo and has a son by him."

"Um...she was living with a Canadian, and they have a five-year-old son, but the guy's way gone."

"And now you're with her? Really? Since when?" Nelly shrieked.

"Shhh, let's not wake the kids."

Nelly grabbed the soap bottle off the sink and threw it at Toro, who ducked. "Now you're worried about our children?" she screamed. "Since when, Toro?"

"Nelly. Calm down."

"Calm down? You loser! Calm down? Why? You've been with another woman for God knows how long. She's pregnant. You want me to calm down?"

"It hasn't been that long...maybe six months...off and on."

"Six months? So you not coming home until early morning hours wasn't 'work'...it was you screwing Sandy? Is that it?" she shrieked.

Toro reached out to take Nelly into his arms, wanting to ease her pain. "I'm sorry. I got caught up in it."

Nelly jerked away. "What does that mean? You trying to say this wasn't your *fault*? Get away from me. Get out! Get out! I can't even look at you!"

"Mommy, are you okay?" a sleepy Jessica asked, padding into the kitchen and rubbing her eyes. "Mommy? Why are you crying?"

Nelly turned her back on Toro and bent down to gather Jessica in her arms.

Toro walked out the front door, slamming it behind him.

⊰

Nelly awoke early after a restless night. Over and over she'd imagined Toro in Sandy's arms—in Sandy's bed. That vivid scene in her mind's eye sliced through her like a dull knife, the pain unbearable. After staring at her reflection in the bathroom mirror, Nelly fought back tears and splashed cold water on her red, swollen eyes.

What am I going to do? Leave him? Where would I go? To my mom's? She has Daniel and Veronica and Ruben's kids. There's no room for three more.

Nelly walked into the kitchen to make coffee. She stood at the kitchen sink and thought about her options, her heart breaking into little pieces.

Within moments, Esteben's girlfriend, Lucia, joined her. "Are you gonna be okay, Nelly?" she asked, combing her manicured nails through waist-length brown hair.

"No. I'm not. My world is crumbling at my feet. How can I be okay? My life is over."

"I'm so sorry this is happening." Compassion filled Lucia's dark eyes.

Collapsing into a chair at the kitchen table, Nelly held her face in her hands and sobbed, unable to control her hurt.

"Something will happen to set things right, Nelly."

"Did you know, Lucia? Did you know about Toro and Sandy? Am I the last one to know? Are people in the Barrio laughing behind my back?"

"I didn't know until Esteben told me last night over at Julio's house. What are you going to do?"

Nelly squared her shoulders and dried her tears with the sleeve of her robe. "I've been thinking about that for hours, Lucia. And you know what? I'm not going anywhere. This is my home. I've lived with Toro for nine years. We have two children. I've helped build this empire of his by keeping our children safe and sound and not complaining about his late night partying and 'business dealings.' I've packed up and moved us from house to house. I've protected him from himself in his binges and rages. He owes me!"

Furious, Nelly rose from her chair. "He needs to decide. Me or her. And I'm not leaving."

"So, what's your plan?" Lucia asked. "How can I help?"

"Will you wake the kids in an hour? Drive Felipe to school and take care of Jessica for a few hours?"

"Sure. Where are you going?"

"I'm not sure. I just have to get out of here for a bit."

"Okay. You do what you need to do," Lucia said, hugging her sister-in-law. "And, Nelly, I'm so sorry. You don't deserve this."

Nelly rushed to change into blue jeans and a sleeveless blouse. *I have to get out of this house.* She tied her long hair into a bun at the base of her neck and slipped her feet into sandals. Grabbing her purse and car keys off the kitchen table, she marched out the door.

Angry and determined, Nelly drove down a dusty road near the town cemetery a few minutes later. *I know the tramp lives somewhere in this area.* She slowed her vehicle and rounded the corner at the end of the road. There it was. Unmistakable. Toro's big white truck parked outside a two-story yellow house. She froze...not wanting to face the truth.

Despite herself, she couldn't stop staring. At the truck. At the house. At the truth. Gulping back tears, she drove on, no longer ignoring the sinking feeling in her stomach. *He's here. With her.*

❧

Toro returned home before two o'clock, in time for lunch. He parked his truck, gathered his resolve, and entered the house. He glanced at Nelly in the kitchen who was ignoring him. Jessica and Felipe came running. "Papi!"

"Run outside and play for a moment while your mom finishes preparing lunch. Go."

As the kids slammed the door behind them, Toro approached Nelly. "Nelly?"

No response.

"Do you want to talk about this?"

No reply.

Toro grabbed a bottle of Corona from the fridge and settled in at the table. "I'll wait."

Nelly slammed the frying pan down on the counter. "Talk about what?"

"Us."

"Us? You want to talk about 'us' now? Isn't it a bit late? You should have thought about 'us' before you hooked up with Sandy."

Toro saw her fighting back tears and felt punched in the gut.

"You need to decide between me and her, Toro Rivera. But so you know. I'm not leaving this house. This is my home."

Teeth clenched, the muscles in his jaw flexing, Toro stared at her. "I'm not choosing."

"What? What do you mean you're not choosing?" Nelly yelled.

"I want you and Sandy. I'm not choosing, so you both need to deal with it. Or leave." Strolling to the refrigerator, Toro pulled another beer from the refrigerator, walked out the door, got into his truck and sped away.

Nelly curled into a fetal position on the sofa and wept.

"Mommy, why are you sad?" Jessica asked a few minutes later, sitting down next her mother. "Don't cry." She patted her mother's knee.

Lucia walked in and found Nelly shaking uncontrollably. "Nelly, what happened?" she asked, sitting on the sofa's arm rest.

Nelly didn't answer.

Lucia rushed to turn the burner off under the pot of rice before it burned. "Jessica, honey, go outside and play with Felipe. Your mommy doesn't feel good. Let me talk to her."

Jessica, fear and confusion clouding her young face, nodded and left the house.

"Nelly, pull yourself together. What's going on?"

"It's Toro," Nelly stammered through sobs.

"What about him? Where is he? What happened now?"

"He left...probably to *her* house." Nelly's chest heaved as her sobs deepened.

"What her? Sandy?"

"Yes."

"Okay, calm down. Take a deep breath and talk to me. Tell me what happened."

"He came home and told me...told me...that he's not going to choose. He wants both of us. I live with his decision or leave."

"*Desgraciado!*" Lucia swore, holding her sister-in-law. "What a self-righteous idiot."

❧CHAPTER SIXTEEN❧

S tart packing," Toro said walking into the house on a warm March afternoon in 2010, three months after his ultimatum.

"We're moving."

"Moving? Moving where?" Nelly asked, confusion clouding her face.

"Over to your parent's house."

"My parent's house? Why? What are you thinking, Toro?"

"Your mom owes me money and she can't pay. That house is her collateral."

"You're kicking my parents out of their house? Our family home? Toro!"

"Stop your whining, Nelly. She will never pay me back the thousands of pesos she's borrowed over the last year. This way she'll be free of the debt."

"You're going to kick my parents and siblings onto the street? Where will they go? You can't do this, Toro. How mean can you be?"

"I could be that mean, but I'm not. The renters in the house behind the school are leaving. Your family will move there. We'll rent this house and move into their place. It's bigger, with room to add on. And it's closer to town."

With a satisfied smile, Toro got comfortable on the leather sofa. "I'm going into the beer business."

Nelly crumpled into the adjacent easy chair and caught her breath. *I'm twenty-three, living with a man I don't know anymore. Virgin Mary, Mother of Jesus, help me. I've lost the strength to fight him.*

"Okay," Nelly said, resigned, a few moments later. "I'll have Lucia help. They're going with us, right?"

"Yes. Esteben will be in charge of the beer store."

"Why do you want to sell beer? Don't you have enough money coming in?"

"There's never enough money, Nelly. Get real. The beer delivery will be a cover-up for the drug deliveries. Ricky is coming to live with us and will arrive by bus in a couple of days. He'll help Miguel and Julio make deliveries on motorcycles. It's a great idea. Nobody will know."

"Why do you feel you need to hide suddenly? The police don't touch you—they're on your payroll."

Toro moved over to the easy chair and attempted to squeeze his large frame in next to Nelly. Unable to fit, he maneuvered her onto his lap, put his arms around her waist and savored the feel of her. *I hate this emotional 'war zone' between us. I wish we were the same Toro and Nelly we were in the beginning—young, idealistic and in love. Will she ever forgive me?*

"It's complicated, Nelly," Toro said, turning her to sit on one knee so he could see her face. "I prefer to keep you out of the scary details...but a few weeks ago, all the cartels aligned in two factions. On one side are the Juarez, Tijuana, and Beltra-Leyva cartels along with Los Zetas. On the other side are the Gulf, Sinaloa and La Familia cartels."

"So? What does that have to do with us?" she asked.

"It's like a civil war of drug cartels," he explained. "It shows the huge push for control of all Mexico. And if La Familia falls, I'm at risk."

Toro saw his words pierce her. Then his heart swelled with love as she laid her head on his shoulder, something she hadn't done in months. *I've missed our closeness.*

"Just get out, Toro. Please? Just walk away. We have enough money and things to live comfortably for the rest of our lives."

He kissed her temple. "It's not that easy, amorcita. You don't just walk away in this business. Somebody will eventually come for me. It's best to stay put, have people around me I can trust, and keep a very low profile."

"But motorcycle deliveries?"

"Yes. It's genius. Our trucks are too well known. Now they won't be seen around the local towns as much. People will just see boys on motorcycles delivering beer. The three bikes I ordered today will be ready for pickup in Vallarta next week. Get packing! We have work to do."

Toro set Nelly aside in the chair and strolled into the kitchen to look into the cooking pots, smelling the aroma of pulled pork.

"Do my parents know you're moving them out?" Nelly asked with sadness in her voice.

"Yes, I talked to your mother earlier. She, Lupita, and Veronica are already packing."

"You didn't tell my father? Isn't that disrespectful?"

"He's not the one who borrowed money, Nelly. She did. Let's go. You need to start packing. Get Felipe to help you."

"But Toro. You're not thinking this through."

"Of course I am. Didn't I just finish explaining it to you? What aren't you getting?"

"We're moving from a remote area with no neighbors to a house with neighbors on both sides."

"I know that," Toro said.

"And not just any neighbors. They're both Americans. Gloria lives on one side and Rebecca on the other."

"So...what's your point?"

"They're not going to take kindly to a lot of noise...especially Rebecca."

Toro opened the door to leave. "Let her be bothered. I don't care. Who's she going to complain to? The police?"

PART TWO ~ REBECCA & TORO

2010 – 2013

❧CHAPTER SEVENTEEN❧

November, 2010

After closing the Bible, I leaned back into the chair cushions and felt the implications of the message I'd received from God. "Love thy neighbor."

"I understand the concept, God," I said. "But do you know who my neighbor is? Nelly and the kids are sweet, but Toro? How can I love him when I'm afraid of him?"

Toro's massive body and stony face intimidated me. I'd been told he was only twenty-five. He looked ten years older.

"Guide me, Lord," I whispered as I left the house a few hours later.

Next door, Toro lay in a hammock strung between two pine trees near the front door of his house. Near him, his two children sat on the cement slab, playing.

"Rebecca!" Felipe left his toy cars behind and rushed to wrap his arms around my legs.

"Rebecca!" Jessica squealed as she grabbed her Barbie doll and followed her brother.

"*Hola, amores,*" I said, gathering four-year-old Jessica into my arms. Jessica's long, raven-black hair caressed my face. Her dark-as-night eyes sparkled with delight.

Jessica reached up and touched my red curly hair. "I like your hair," she said in her sweet voice.

"And I like yours," I replied, smiling.

I pulled Felipe close with my free arm. Toro's seven-year-old son was small for his age. His eyes seemed to reflect more disquiet than delight. Each time I saw him, I could tell he longed for attention. I was happy to give it.

"Can we swim at your house today, Rebecca? Please? Please?" Felipe asked.

I looked toward their father, who remained comatose in his hammock. *Probably still hung over from all the partying that kept me awake last night.*

Anger against Toro and all he stood for wanted to rob me of another day where I would walk around complaining about not sleeping or not being able to enjoy my home. I steeled myself and instead gave Felipe a big hug. "Not today, honey. I'm just walking into town for the afternoon, but let me talk to your mom tonight about you coming to swim tomorrow."

"Okay. Don't forget," Felipe said, hanging his head.

I kissed and set sweet-smelling Jessica gently down, smiled and walked away. *I can do this. I can face my fear and be a blessing to these children. I may not approve of Toro, but they are not at fault for the sins of their father.*

❧

130

I spent the afternoon with my sister, Tina, at her house in town. Tina had lived in La Perlita full time for over thirty years.

She was married to Joaquin, a local Mexican. Over a glass of wine, we talked about my fear to obey the mandate, "love thy neighbor."

"He used to work for Joaquin, years ago," Tina said.

"Was he always this scary?" I laughed.

"I didn't know him, but Joaquin liked him. He says he was a good worker."

"Then I'll let Joaquin move to my house and he can 'love my neighbor.' I'll move in here with you."

Tina poured us another glass of wine. "It took Joaquin over ten years to build your house. I don't think you'll move out."

"You're right, Sis. I won't."

૰

I made my way back home a few hours later. Nearing the house, I noticed Nelly working in the beer store, located right on the adjoining wall of their house and my privacy wall. The store measured ten square feet. Boxes of beer were stacked from floor to ceiling on two sides of the room, with a glass-door refrigerator on the far wall, behind a waist-high counter.

"*Buenas tardes, Nelly. ¿Cómo estas?*"

Nelly shut the refrigerator door. "*Hola*, Rebecca."

I gave Nelly a hug. "It's good to see you. Your kids sure have grown. I can remember holding little Jessica before she could walk."

"They're growing too fast," Nelly said, wiping down the countertop. "Are you going to be here long?"

"Until late March," I answered. "By the way, can the kids swim at my house tomorrow?"

"Thank you for the invite, but Toro doesn't let the children out of our sight. Unless they're with family."

"Veronica and Daniel are your family. Would Toro allow it if they come too?"

"Possibly. I can't make those decisions. Let me talk to him tonight and I'll let you know."

"Great. And if you don't mind my asking...when I left for the States last March, your parents, little sister and brother, and your brother Ruben's three kids lived here. This was your family home. What changed?"

Nelly paused.

I waited, wondering about the hesitation.

"Toro had a house a few blocks further into the Barrio," she finally said. "He offered it to my parents. They moved over there and we moved here, renting out our other place. This is a better location. We're only a half block from the main road into town."

Nelly took a moment to wait on a young boy who came into the store to buy chips and soda. "His brothers can make faster beer deliveries on their motorcycles from here."

"That makes sense," I said, holding back my complaints about the late-night motorcycle noise. "I've known your family for over four years. Your younger siblings along with Ruben's three kids are used to swimming at my place. I hope Toro will allow Felipe and Jessica to join them."

"We'll see. Veronica and Daniel love being at your house."

"I like them being there, too. Did they mention they have to pay to swim?"

Nelly looked surprised.

"Yes. I give them a jumbo-sized trash bag and they have to bring it back to me full of empty bottles and trash they've picked up in the neighborhood."

Nelly laughed. I noticed her dimples and realized again how beautiful she was and how much Jessica looked like her.

"That sounds fair. I'll call my mom and see if Veronica and Daniel are available. Ruben's three kids don't live with my parents anymore. They moved back to live with their mother up near Guadalajara."

"Oh, okay. I'll miss them, but I'm glad they're with their mom. Adios, see you later."

⮞

Nelly's younger sister and brother weren't available to swim the following day, and Toro didn't allow his children to visit alone. *Maybe he doesn't want them in the pool?*

I was determined to "love thy neighbor" starting with Toro's children, so I tried another tactic. *Ice cream. I'll ask if Jessica and Felipe can walk into town with Daniel, Veronica, and me for ice cream.*

Toro again refused, through Nelly.

"He won't let me take his kids anywhere," I complained to my brother-in-law, a few days after Nelly reluctantly rejected my ice cream invitation.

Joaquin smiled in his gruff kind of way. "Toro used to work for me in construction when he was just a kid. Right after his family packed up and moved back to Michoacán."

"Yeah, Tina mentioned that."

"He's a decent guy. Power and money have gone to his head though. I'd bet he's afraid to let the kids out of the house with a stranger. A rival drug gang could snatch them away from you."

"What? A rival drug gang? What are you talking about?" I settled down next to Joaquin on the curb in front of his and Tina's house. "Who would want to kidnap Toro's kids?"

"I just told you...a rival drug gang."

"That doesn't make any sense, Joaquin. This is a small fishing village. Not some big city where things like that happen."

Joaquin rose to leave. "You're a bit naïve, Rebecca."

"I've heard Toro sells drugs. That doesn't shock me, Joaquin. Back in the early '70s during my wanna-be-a-hippy days, I lived with a drug dealer. There was no rival drug gang after him."

"This is different, Rebecca. Just be aware," he said walking into the house.

≈

Curious, I spoke to my friend, Chato a retired police officer. Chato came from a long-standing La Perlita family. I had met him through my sister Tina when I was seventeen and Chato was in his mid-twenties.

134

"Toro isn't just a guy who sells drugs," Chato told me. "He's also in charge of others who sell all kinds of narcotics up and down the coast. There's a lot money involved. If a rival cartel wants to take over this area, they will attack. I'm sure he's afraid his children could be kidnapped to get to him."

Chato leaned back in his rocking chair and crossed his ankles. "There have been thousands of drug-related killings and more than ten thousand people have gone missing since President Calderon took office four years ago. It's a scary time for Mexico. Rival cartels are fighting for each other's territories."

I shook my head in disbelief. My heart constricted. *Who am I living next to?* "Chato, I've been told he's only twenty-five," I said. "That's younger than my son, Fernando."

Chato nodded. "He may be young in years, but he's not your normal twenty-five-year-old. He's had to be ruthless to stay on top. He does have his enemies."

"How dangerous is it that the cartels are scrambling for new territory? For him, for us, for La Perlita?" I asked, confused and concerned.

"He's most likely affiliated with La Familia Cartel in Michoacán. At least that's what buddies of mine in law enforcement tell me. That cartel is powerful, so he should be okay. Reports are they have the firepower and logistical support to wage war. They murdered twelve federal police in Michoacán a year ago and another ten this year."

"They kill federal cops?" I asked, thinking about how dangerous that would be in the States. "All hell breaks loose if you kill a police officer in the States, Chato."

"Unfortunately it's a daily occurrence here, Rebecca. I don't want to scare you, but the cartel assassins kill authorities and they execute rival cartel members. They keep extending their territory of control using violence and fear."

Chato's wife, Marta, came into the living room with a smile on her sweet round face. "Welcome back, amiga," she said, handing me a glass of iced tea and coconut cookies.

"Oh, gracias, Marta. It's good to see you." I planted a kiss on her cheek. "Join us. We're talking about the drug cartels and Toro Rivera, my new neighbor."

"I overheard from the kitchen," Marta replied, adjusting her eyeglasses. "We're a small village. I know Toro. We all know Toro. I heard he moved into Lidia and Roberto's house next to you."

I grimaced. "Yep, he's my new neighbor. Do you want to exchange houses?"

Marta laughed. "No, we're good here."

Chato accepted iced tea from his wife. "Toro isn't all bad. He helps people by loaning them money."

"Really? There's something good about Toro?" I asked Chato.

"There is. And, I understand there have been times he's even protected our community by punishing wrongdoers himself."

"Isn't punishment the job of the police or judicial system?"

Chato stretched out his legs. "It should be, but the wheels of justice are known to move way too slow. Toro settles things quickly...at least that's what I've heard. He controls with a strong hand. But he does control."

A while later, I rose to leave, kissing Chato and Marta goodbye. As I turned toward the door, Chato said, "Toro must know mafia groups are fighting for control of the Jalisco coast. They're putting their own people into drug-selling zones, called *plazas*. Maybe he's concerned they'll come after him. That's got to be why he's so protective of his family."

Days passed as Chato's words swirled inside my head. I battled with my fears and faith. Maybe God didn't give me the mandate to love my neighbor. Maybe that was just one of my own crazy thoughts.

To avoid meeting up with Toro in front of his house, I walked a different route into town. I used a well-worn path through the coconut groves and crossed the paved streets in the El Tropical subdivision where Americans and Canadians had built homes.

This neighborhood could exist anywhere along the Pacific coast. Modern two-story homes painted in earth tones. Beach views from palapa-roof bars on the third-floor. Homeowner's association. Cars parked behind secure wrought-iron fences. Hmmm. If I lived here, Toro wouldn't be my neighbor!

Weeks went by. The loud music, noise, and smell of the goats continued. Motorcycles roared up and down the street at night— delivering beer and most likely drugs. Night after night I lay awake, missing the old days when barking dogs and roosters without a sense of time were the only things keeping me awake.

How can I make this stop?

Then it happened.

❧CHAPTER EIGHTEEN↤

The deafening cherry-bomb-like explosion went off at six in the morning, shaking the bedroom windows, jerking me six inches up off the mattress and scaring the beejezus out of me. I exhaled, calmed my nerves, and pulled the covers over my head, willing myself to go back to sleep.

Another bomb exploded.

"Here we go," I muttered. I'd spent enough winters in Mexico to know the "bombs" would explode every half hour for the next two hours—an announcement by the priest and his staff at the Barrio church, reminding everyone that Catholic Mass on holy days began at 7:00 a.m. sharp.

Yep, it's the twelfth, the birthday of the Virgin de Guadalupe. No sleeping in today. Why can't the kindly priest just ring a church bell? Does he think we're deaf?

I threw the sheets off and plodded upstairs to the kitchen to make coffee and chase the cobwebs from my tired head.

Well, at least I'll see the sunrise for once.

I took my coffee outside to sit on the upstairs balcony which faced south, allowing me to see sunrises by looking to my left and sunsets by looking to my right.

Another loud explosion erupted. I jumped and then laughed, remembering what I'd told my Canadian friend, Cal, the year before when *he* complained about the priest's wake-up calls on holy days. "What explosions?" I'd asked, feigning innocence. "I don't hear anything. Only sinners hear the bombs on holy days."

The sudden "could-it-be-true?" expression on his face made me laugh aloud.

The day of the *Virgin de Guadalupe* became a Mexican national holiday in 1859. The country celebrates with fervor. Local friends had told me the story years earlier of how the Virgin Mary appeared to a poor indigenous man, Juan Diego, on December 9 and again on December 12, 1531. She asked him to have the bishop build a temple on the spot where she appeared, Tepeyac Hill, to receive petitions and heal the suffering of the Mexican people.

In the sleepy beach town of La Perlita devout Catholics attend Mass on the Virgin of Guadalupe day. Later, hundreds parade through town singing and reenacting the story of Juan Diego and his miraculous encounters with La Virgin.

I looked forward to the yearly parade. Schoolchildren dressed in peasant attire walk behind a teacher dressed as Juan Diego, who carries a four-foot high replica of La Virgin de Guadalupe. A float, decorated with red and yellow roses, transports an eight-foot-high statute of La Virgin. Men dressed in bright colored Aztec costumes bang on drums and dance along the parade route, while parishioners representing Aztec women carry flowers, candles, and a variety of La Virgin pictures.

The not-so-devout spend their days and nights partying and setting off firecrackers. And, since December 12 is in the middle of Advent, the time leading up to Christmas, the Virgin of Guadalupe's birthday sets off the non-stop Christmas party season, including the firecrackers that explode at all hours.

Later that morning, I swallowed my fear and passed by Toro's house on my way into town to see the parade. Felipe, Daniel, and Veronica huddled in the middle of the dusty street with a variety of firecrackers. Daniel held a cigarette lighter in his hand ready to light the next one.

"Watch out, Rebecca!" eleven-year-old Veronica called.

As a rocket whizzed toward me, I scrambled to my right. I almost slammed into Toro, who was leaning against the beer-store door.

"Sorry," I blurted.

Toro nodded.

I smelled alcohol reeking from his body. Without thinking, I reached out and touched a welt on his forearm. "What happened? Did you get too near a firecracker?"

"The wrench slipped when I was fixing Felipe's bike."

With a confidence that surprised me, I again touched his arm. "Have Nelly put antibacterial ointment on that. It doesn't look good."

Toro stayed silent, his facial expression unmoving. He took a sip of his beer.

I backed up and walked away.

Well. That wasn't so bad. I touched him, I spoke to him, and I didn't faint or anything.

❧

The next opportunity to "love thy neighbor" came just before Christmas. Toro, Nelly, and several dozen friends partied outside their house as my friend, Katherine and I walked home from town.

"This is different," Katherine said. "I've never seen so many people on your street before."

Katherine had arrived from California the day before to visit for a week. We had enjoyed a scrumptious dinner of chicken fajitas at the Sea Master Restaurant while watching a gorgeous orange and red sunset. Full and content, we looked forward to settling in at my house for a Netflix movie.

As we approached the party, I noticed plates of rice, beans, pulled pork, and barbecued chicken covering round plastic tables set out on the street. Adults drank, children played, firecrackers exploded, and the music blared.

Another sleepless night.

"Don't you drink with your neighbors?" Toro called, as I maneuvered my way through the tables and hugged the kids who came running.

"Sure I do," I answered. *Don't do this.* On impulse, I walked up to Toro, removed the drink from his hand and took a big sip of what I hoped was a margarita. I choked on pure tequila.

I coughed and Toro laughed when I handed him back his plastic glass. "Not bad, Gringa," he said. "Not bad."

I walked on, feeling somewhat foolish, but proud of myself for swallowing my fear along with the tequila.

"That was brave," Katherine whispered, rounding the corner to the patio door.

"I don't know what came over me. Now my throat burns. That was pure tequila—at least I think it was tequila. It was strong."

Katherine chuckled, her blue eyes full of merriment—or maybe it was disbelief at my brazenness.

∽

"What's with these new neighbors of yours?" Katherine asked later as we settled into the upstairs living room. "Are they always this noisy?"

"Yep. Unfortunately."

"What do you know about them?" she asked.

"I know Toro manages drug dealers up and down the coast. He's powerful. From what I've gleaned from friends and taxi drivers, he's liked by some. Feared by others. His brothers and nephews deliver beer on motorcycles—as you heard last night. I think the beer is a front for the drug sales."

"He's scary looking," Katherine said. "I wouldn't want to meet up with him in a dark alley."

"Me either. Nelly and the kids are sweet. That's a good thing."

"Do you think he's dangerous or just scary?"

In a futile attempt to drown out the noise from next door, I turned up the television volume. "I've heard that one of his drug dealers tried to steal money from him. Soon after, that dealer went 'missing.'"

"Oh, no. That's not good. And he's your neighbor."

"You got it. I'm not moving. I'll figure out how to love my unlovable neighbor—while praying he moves away soon."

∽

The following morning, Katherine and I gathered in the living room enjoying a cup of coffee. Just as Katherine stood up to walk into the kitchen, what sounded like rounds from a machine gun reverberated through the open windows.

"Duck!" Katherine screamed and hit the ground.

"It's okay, Katherine," I said without moving. "We're safe. It's early morning firecrackers."

∽

Morning, Son, I texted to my twenty-seven-year-old son, Fernando on New Year's Eve.

Gud mornin, Mommy, Fernando texted back.

My fingers tapped the tiny keyboard of my phone. *I need u 2 pray 4 me 2day.*

Watsup?

I invited Toro to come over. He's coming 2day at 4.

U wat?? Hold on. I'll call u!

Moments later, I answered my son's phone call from thirteen hundred miles away in Arizona. He didn't waste words. "What are you thinking? Why have Toro come to the house?"

"Because this noise and parties and beer deliveries at night have to stop," I said. "I can't sleep. I call the cops when the partying is still going after midnight. They stop by, and then the racket continues after they leave."

"Talk to him at his house. Or out on the street."

"No, I want it to be here, where we can sit in the shade and talk with nobody around."

"That's my concern, Mom. Nobody else around."

"It'll be okay. Ever since the evening I choked on his tequila, he says *hola* when I walk by. I even saw him smile once."

"Isn't your friend Katherine there? You should have someone with you."

"No. I waited until she left to have this meeting with Toro."

"Mom. Why? Geez! I don't like this."

"I'll be okay. Just pray for me. It's become obvious neither of us are going anywhere, so we need an agreement—of some sort."

"Oh, Mom."

"Son, nobody is going to help me here. I'm obeying God to love my neighbor."

I paced around the yard with the phone to my ear, feeling the damp grass under my bare feet. "Katherine has visited me for the last couple of years and loves it here. This time, we both had to take sleeping pills and use ear plugs. That's not okay."

"I understand, Mom. But I worry for your safety. Your friends in town told you Toro's part of a drug cartel. That's scary stuff. I don't think it's a good thing to tick him off."

I heard my son sigh. "It's two o'clock there, right? That gives you two hours to change your mind—or not. Call me when he leaves."

"I will. I love you, Son."

ᔂCHAPTER NINETEENᔄ

I heard the knock—the tinny tapping of car keys on the metal security door.

Taking a deep breath, I opened the door to Toro, a smile on my face. "*Buenas tardes*, Toro. Thanks for coming."

He nodded.

I noted his snug Levi jeans, a short-sleeved striped shirt buttoned almost to the top, and huaraches on his feet. His stomach overflowed his belt.

I left the patio door open, and escorted Toro down the tiled corridor, past the brick arches and pillars, and invited him to sit on a cushioned chair underneath the outdoor fan.

He looked around, and then glanced right, to the north-side privacy wall. Using a ladder, he could climb up my side of the wall, move aside the bougainvillea vines, and jump down ten feet onto his back patio. That's how close we lived to each other.

I knew his younger brother, Ricky had scurried down the wall into my yard the day before, using the trunk of a palm tree for leverage. I watched him from an upstairs window. He collected a soccer ball and then hustled back up. His dirty shoe prints still marred the cream-colored wall. I didn't mention Ricky's visit.

"Nice place."

"Thanks," I replied.

"I used to play here when this house was being built," Toro said. "My family lived across the street."

I knew the house he was referring to—small, old, unkempt, and now sitting empty.

His memory of being a kid and playing on my property, and now telling me about it, made him kind of "human."

I smiled. "That would have been the first build of this house. Before the earthquake of '95. The doors and windows weren't even in. I ended up tearing it down and starting again because of damage to the foundation. How old were you then?"

"Ten. I played here with my brothers after school. That was before my father took me out of school. To work."

I didn't know his story, but I felt sad for him, for the pain I detected in his eyes before he looked away.

"My brother-in-law Joaquin built this house," I explained. "It took him ten years, because I never had enough money to build start to finish. He tore down the first house, dug deep and put massive cement footings in the ground, and then started the rebuild."

"We all used to think this was Don Joaquin's house," Toro said. "We didn't realize he was building it for you until you moved in."

I chuckled. "I've heard that before, from taxi drivers bringing me home. Everybody thought this was *Casa de Joaquin*. He sure built it to last, like it was his."

This is going well. I inhaled and exhaled to calm my nerves.

"Would you like a drink? I have wine."

"No, thanks. I drank too much last night."

Ya think? I wanted to say, remembering the hoots and hollers, the loud, lively, foot-stomping, Mexican music peppered with "ahahaaaayyy!" until 2:00 a.m.

Before I could respond, Felipe slipped through the open patio door and ran over to sit next to me. I hugged him and kissed his forehead.

"Can I go into the pool?" he asked.

His father gave him a stern look.

"Well, first I want to take your dad to see the house inside. You can come with us and when we come back down, you can put your feet in the water by the steps. If it's okay with your dad," I added, looking at Toro.

Toro nodded approval.

Take him up to see the house? Really?

I did.

Toro and Felipe followed me up the circular stairs to the front door. I showed them the spacious open area of living room, kitchen, and dining room. After pausing for them to peek into my office, I led them down the hallway to the bedrooms, one on each side.

"If you look out the window in this room," I told Toro, pushing aside the pale blue curtains in the room facing his house, "you can almost see your goats."

He stayed silent.

"I want to see," Felipe said. His father lifted him up to look out the window.

Father and son followed me down the inside stairwell to the master bedroom and then out the large French doors to the patio.

"Can I get my feet in the water now?" Felipe asked.

"*Sí*," I said, settling on the patio chair.

I watched Felipe remove his sandals and splash his feet in the pool.

"I asked you to come by today, Toro, because I have a few concerns I think you can help me resolve."

"What are your concerns?" he asked, looking surprised.

You! I wanted to say. "Well, things seem a bit noisy since I arrived this season. And I'm wondering if we can work something out."

He sat, silent.

I lowered my voice. "I respect your right to live the way you want, but as your neighbor I'm affected by your choices."

His face remained etched in stone, so I continued. "I've replaced the upstairs windows in those bedrooms you saw, the ones facing your house. But, the late night pounding from your stereo system still shakes my house. And the goats out back? They stink. And your dogs bark all night."

"I didn't realize it bothered you," he said.

"I wish it didn't, but it does, Toro. This is my paradise home." I looked around the yard at the palm trees, bright flowers, and pool. "I look forward to spending time here. But now, I don't feel so much in paradise, especially since I'm sleep deprived."

"Felipe! Don't go into the water. Sit back down or go home," Toro shouted at his son.

Felipe obeyed while I prayed for strength to continue our conversation, not wanting Toro's quick anger directed at me.

"When I come home from town at night, I have to wonder what you're up to, because *you* decide if I sleep or not." I smiled to take the sting off my words.

"Is there something else bothering you?" he asked, not giving me a clue to his feelings about my complaints.

I hurried through the list in my head. "Well...yes. Your brothers are delivering beer all night. I hear the phone ring with the order, and then it's 'clang, clang, clang' as they roll up the metal door, then 'clink, clink, clink' as they put beer and ice into the coolers, and then more 'clang, clang, clang' as they lower the door. And then comes the roar of their motorcycles as they drive off. As you know, this happens all night. I'm shocked that people order cases of beer at three in the morning."

"Anything else?"

Anything else? How much more do you need? "No," I replied and settled back in my chair, crossing my arms.

After hesitating a minute, Toro said, "The dogs are barking because their job is to protect the goats from thieves. There's a horse in the lot behind the goat corral and anytime the horse comes near, the dogs bark."

I nodded, not wanting him to stop talking now that he'd started.

"I brought the dogs and the goats here, because we left them corralled outside my place further out in the Barrio, and several were stolen. I need them close."

"Makes sense," I said, seeing I was most likely going to lose this battle.

"The stench is coming from lack of clean-up in the corral. My young cousin, Chuche, is in charge of the goats. He's to walk them twice a day, so they can eat grass around the neighborhood. And it's his job to keep the corral clean."

"I see him walking them," I responded.

"Felipe! Let's go," Toro said.

You're leaving? You haven't resolved my issues! "Well, thank you for coming," I said, escorting him to the door.

Felipe, sandals in hand, followed. "Papá, can I stay here with Rebecca?"

"No. Let's go!"

As Toro started through the doorway, I reached out and touched his arm. "Toro, I respect you. I trust you can do something about the things we talked about today. Thank you."

He nodded and walked away.

Felipe, head down, trudged out the door behind him.

❧CHAPTER TWENTY❧

After closing the patio door, I climbed into my white hammock hanging between two of the brick pillars and took a deep breath.

Well, I didn't get what I wanted, but I think there was a break-through with Toro. Maybe.

I called Fernando. "Hi, Son."

"Hey, Mom. I've been waiting for your call. All okay?"

"It went okay. I talked. He listened. He shared a bit. I'm still alive."

After listening to me tell him every detail of my visit with Toro, Fernando said, "At least you're safe. That's good. Now what?"

"I don't know. I'll just wait and see. By the way, happy New Year's Eve, Son."

"Happy New Year's Eve, Mom. I'll call you at midnight your time. Will you be home?"

"No, I'll be at Tina and Joaquin's for a party. Better there than the noise and crowds I'll be facing here. Someday I'll get up my nerve and join Toro and his parties rather than resent them."

"That sounds like something you'd do, Mom. But don't be fooled. Drug dealers at Toro's level are dangerous and people that hang around with him shouldn't be trusted either."

"I'm playing the naïve American neighbor, honey," I said. "Toro doesn't know I know he's a drug dealer. But, even so, I'll be careful, Son. Love you."

∽

Two weeks into 2011, I awoke late to a realization: *I slept all night! What happened? Did Toro move?*

I inhaled as I walked up the inside stairs. *Hmmm, no goats smell to flavor my morning coffee. Maybe he did move.* Pushing aside the curtains in the upstairs bedroom, I peered down into the goat corral partially hidden behind Toro's back privacy wall. *What? No goats. No dogs. Maybe Chuche is walking them early...or maybe Toro **is** gone.*

My fantasies of a life without Toro's intrusions came to a sudden halt when I spotted him with Felipe and Jessica in the empty lot on the south side of my house. Toro had thrown a thick rope over a branch of the old fig tree and was attaching a used tire for a swing. Felipe and Jessica looked up, saw me, and waved.

"*Buenos dias,*" I greeted the three.

"*Buenos dias*, Rebecca," the kids responded in unison.

Toro is across the street? Ten months earlier, I had grown tired of the trash and weeds in that lot, a direct view from my balcony. I decided to have it cleaned. I wanted a place for the neighborhood children to play, and a better view for myself.

154

The absentee owner, the same one who hadn't responded to any of my phone calls about the eyesore, had shown up a few days into the clean-up project. "He may not be responding to your attempts to make contact, Rebecca," my gardener, Francisco, had predicted, "but believe me, the moment we start cutting weeds and clearing debris, someone will notify him."

And sure enough, a large black truck with a *"Viva Guadalajara"* sticker on the bumper appeared as if by magic the day the workers and I raked dried brush to burn it.

"Excuse me," the tall, middle-aged man said, stepping down from his truck. "This is my father's land you're clearing."

"*Hola.* I'm your neighbor, Rebecca. The land office gave me your family's phone number last year. You haven't responded to any of my messages."

We shook hands. "Sorry. We received them. Something about garbage, rats, and termites? We live in Guadalajara. A cousin called me yesterday about your cleanup. Do you want to buy this lot? It was for sale a while back. I've brought the land title with me."

"No, I don't. I just want it clean. It's a danger and an eyesore. People come by, see the bags of garbage, think it's a dump, and throw more garbage. I'm tired of cleaning it up for you. I want to plant grass and make a play area for the kids."

The man looked at the work completed and at the faces of the half-dozen children with rakes and shovels who'd shown up to help. "You don't want to buy it?"

"Nope."

He hesitated a few moments. "Okay. Well then...you have my permission to turn it into a park."

"*Gracias.*" I smiled from ear-to-ear.

The kids had cheered at the news.

Now, here was Toro, many months later, adding his touch to the little park. *Progress.*

"*Gracias*, Toro. I like it," I said, loud enough for him to hear. He looked up at me standing on the balcony. I detected a slight smile. That smile I thought I saw prompted me to put on my sandals and walk outside to the park. The kids came running. Toro continued installing the tire swing.

"What happened to the goats...and the dogs?" I asked.

"Chuche herded them back to our other house. He and Ricky will sleep there at nights to make sure none are stolen."

"No wonder it was so quiet this morning. Wait...isn't Ricky one of your beer delivery boys?"

"Yes, but until I figure out the goats, I need him at the other place. I'm hiring another delivery guy."

"What about Esteben? Can't he fill in?" *Geez. What am I doing questioning Toro on his employees? And he's answering me!*

"Esteben has moved on."

"What does that mean?" I asked sitting on a massive root protruding from the base of the fig tree.

Daniel and Veronica arrived on their bikes and joined Felipe and Jessica running around on the grass and up and down the dirt knoll at the edge of the park. *Kids are playing and laughing and I'm talking to Toro. This is different.*

"Esteben's girlfriend, Lucia, just had their second child. They moved into their own place. Lucia doesn't want him delivering beer at all hours, so he got a job managing a construction site."

"How old is he?"

"I'm twenty-five, so he's twenty-three."

Despite myself, I couldn't stop staring at Toro—taking in his thick black hair, chipmunk cheeks and stoic expressions. A handsome young man, but for someone who was only twenty-five he looked so...worn. His dark eyes seemed void of light. I wondered what things he'd seen or done in his line of work.

"It's understandable they want to be on their own," I said as Jessica dived into my lap.

"Can we swim at your house today, Rebecca? Please?" Jessica asked.

"That's up to your dad," I responded.

Felipe, Veronica, and Daniel joined Jessica. They all looked at Toro.

He hesitated.

The kids and I waited.

"Okay," he finally said.

"What time, Rebecca?" Felipe asked, grinning from ear to ear.

"Knock on the patio door at three o'clock to get the trash bags. You can swim when you've finished filling them. Deal?"

"Deal!" four precious children chanted.

Over the weeks, calm came upon the neighborhood. Toro's loud music shut off before midnight and the beer deliveries ceased by two. Toro said nothing about these changes and I didn't ask.

I now looked forward to walking by his house—hoping I'd catch him outside. "Good morning, Toro," I said one morning. "Thanks for letting me sleep last night."

He'd squinted into the morning sun, as if to make sure he had heard me right, before finally nodding. "Mornin."

"Good afternoon, Toro," I announced on another late morning, pushing his hammock as I walked by on my way to the tortilla store. "If you'd get to bed before midnight, you'd be up earlier in the morning." By the time he opened his eyes, I had strolled on up the street.

Teasing him helped me move beyond my fear. Felipe and Jessica enjoyed me pestering their father and joined my banter as I found ways to make him smile.

"*Papá*. Here comes Rebecca, you better wake up," Felipe yelled one morning as he watched me approach.

"*Papá*, Rebecca's here!" Jessica squealed another morning when I stopped to visit Nelly in the beer store.

I smiled as Toro walked out of the house. "Mornin," he said in his gruff way.

"Mornin, Sunshine."

With time, my fear lessened—just a bit, as I began to see signs of a soul smiling back at me on those occasions.

Progress.

ᢙCHAPTER TWENTY-ONEᢍ

In early February, 2011, I propped open the patio door with a brick and began painting the bottom half of the inside privacy wall. Salt from the sea air and the ground water, called *salitre*, gets into bricks and mortar during construction. It easily leaks out and eats through the paint, so every year I cure patches of *salitre* with an anti-salt solution and then repaint.

Halfway through my project, Felipe burst around the corner, bolted through the doorway, and scrambled behind me, holding onto my legs.

"Felipe, *qué pasa amor?*"

"*Mi papá*. He's going to spank me!"

"Spank you? What did you do?"

"*Nada*, Rebecca, *nada*."

Before I could address Felipe's predicament, Toro's massive frame filled the doorway in front of me.

I stood up straight, squaring my shoulders. Given my height of 5'10", I almost stared Toro straight in the eyes.

"Felipe! Get over here," he demanded.

I sensed Felipe's small body trembling. Over the last few months I'd frequently heard Toro's fury directed at Felipe—

followed by Felipe's cries. Standing my ground, I put my arms behind me, touching Felipe and keeping him in place.

"Felipe!"

Without saying a word, I met Toro's stare and then shook my head, as if saying, "Not today, Toro. Not today."

Prepared to receive a direct hit from Toro's anger, I was shocked when he backed up to leave the doorway.

"Just wait 'til you get home, Felipe!" Toro shouted, storming off.

Seconds later, I turned to face little Felipe and bent down to embrace him. "It's okay, amor."

"Can I live here with you, Rebecca? Please?"

"I'm sorry, but no, you can't. Tell me what happened today. Your dad must have a reason for being so angry."

"I didn't do anything. He's *always* angry."

"I can't keep you here, Felipe. You have to face him eventually. Let's go talk to your mom. Okay?"

"Okay. You'll go with me, right?"

"Yes."

Taking Felipe's seven-year-old hand in mine, we walked the short distance from my patio door to his front door. Nelly wasn't in view. Toro walked out of his house as we approached.

I urged Felipe forward. "Go inside with your mom. I'll talk to your dad."

Motioning for Toro to follow me and hoping he would, I crossed the dirt street and sat down on the curb facing our houses. Side by side. Our lives entwined for some God-known reason.

Toro sat down. He crossed his legs at the ankles and his bulky arms across his chest.

"I'm sorry to have interfered today, Toro. He was so scared."

Silence filled the two feet of distance between us.

"What's going on? What has Felipe done to make you so angry?" I asked.

No response.

I waited.

Jessica saw me from the front door and ran across the street to sit on my lap.

Finally, Toro spoke in the silence. "Felipe doesn't listen. Ever. He acts out at school. He doesn't turn in his homework."

Having raised four children of my own, I understood his angst.

I saw darkness cloud his face. "I got called into his school today. Again."

"Let's see. Felipe tells me he's almost eight—so he's in second grade, right?" I asked. "How much homework can he have, and why doesn't he turn it in? Does he finish it?"

"Yes. Then at school today they showed Nelly and me the list of missed work."

"Felipe's in trouble, Rebecca," Jessica said sweetly. "He hit a boy at school."

Surprised, I looked at Toro. "He's hitting other kids?"

"Yes, that's why he deserves a beating."

"You don't know much about me, Toro, but before retirement I worked as a counselor in the States. What I've learned over the years, both professionally and with my own children, is that kids want attention."

Toro didn't respond.

Jessica squirmed out of my arms and ran across the street to play with her dolls.

"You're super busy with your beer business. That's evident by the amount of time your truck is gone. And at night, you're busy with entertaining friends. Right?"

Toro nodded.

"I'm an outsider, but I think Felipe wants attention. Children that don't get positive attention from parents will misbehave to get any attention they can. His bad behavior at school is getting plenty of your attention, right?"

Toro raised an eyebrow. After a few seconds, he replied. "You bet it is."

I smiled. "Exactly. Can you think of ways to spend time with him? Just the two of you?"

He paused for a few seconds. "Maybe."

"That may help," I said. "But if his negative behavior continues, I'm willing to go to school with you or with Nelly to talk with his teacher. Felipe can be a handful, but he's a sweet kid."

I hesitated for a moment waiting for a response. None came.

"Toro. Again, I'm so sorry for interfering today."

"Don't worry about it."

Jessica twirled across the street as I stood to leave. "I'm having a birthday party, Rebecca. Will you come? Please?"

Toro also stood. "Jessica is a Valentine's baby. Her birthday party is Saturday at one. If you'd like to come."

"*Gracias*," I replied. "I'd love to. *Hasta luego*...And, Toro, am I going to sleep tonight?"

He stared at me for a moment. "Maybe," he said with a smirk.

∂CHAPTER TWENTY-TWO∽

February, 2011

Nearly a hundred white plastic chairs trucked in from a party rental company filled the street in front of Toro and Nelly's house. Earlier, from an upstairs window, I had seen the chairs and tables arrive and I'd watched Toro and Miguel string colorful crepe paper decorations and balloons from one side of the street to the other. The preparations and decorations hanging from the corner of my property down a half block to Toro and Nelly's house, heralded the festivities to come.

I strolled toward the party with a new Barbie doll and a set of Barbie clothes wrapped inside a Barbie gift bag.

Near the curb where I'd talked with Toro just a few days prior, I passed Toro and four muscular, scary-looking guys sitting on chairs behind a long wooden table. One had a cross-tattooed under his right eye and another exhibited a red, two-inch scar on his left cheek. A bottle of tequila, limes, and shot glasses sat on the table in front of the men. From the drunken looks on their faces, I figured they'd already started this party.

"*Hola*, Toro," I said, smiling, while my heart beat in fear.

Those guys could chew me up and spit me out.

"Hey, Gringa," Toro slurred and lifted a tequila shot in a toast.

His companions looked at me. My skinned crawled, but my smile remained. *Love thy neighbor.*

"Rebecca," Felipe yelled running towards me.

Relieved by the distraction, I took Felipe's hand and walked closer to the house. *"Hola amor.* Where's the birthday girl?"

"With my mom. Getting dressed."

As if on cue, little Jessica pranced out of the house toward me, dressed in black patent leather shoes, a red and white polka-dot dress with a big matching bow, black ears, and white gloves, looking just like Minnie Mouse.

I swooped her up in my arms, planted a kiss on her cheek, and gave her the gift. *"Feliz cumpleaños, amorcita."*

A clown arrived with loud music and mothers with children soon filled the chairs and tables. A bakery worker delivered two full sheet cakes decorated in red, white, and black, matching Jessica's outfit.

Not that different from a rich child's birthday party in the Unites States.

~

A couple of hours later, with the children's games over and the scary guys gone, I helped Nelly serve bowls of pozole to the guests.

"Rebecca, do you see that woman with a small child? A couple of tables to your left?" she asked.

"Which one?" I responded, seeing multitudes of mothers and children.

"The one with long light-brown hair holding a little boy."

"Yes, who is she?"

"The boy, Marco, is Toro's son, and the woman is his girlfriend."

"Toro's *girlfriend?* His *son?"*

"I hate her," Nelly said with a snarl. "And he brought her here!"

Hearing these words, Nelly's mother, Lidia, motioned for us to enter the house. "*Hija*, you have to accept Marco. Don't blame him for what Toro did. That baby is now part of this family," she said sternly.

"I am Toro's *wife*. We have two children. And he takes another woman? How can I accept that, *Mamá?*"

"You will always be his wife, *Hija*, whether you stood in front of a priest or not. I'm sorry Toro made this decision, but you stand strong and you learn to love that little boy," Lidia said.

My heart shattered listening to Nelly's sadness and seeing the tears spring to her eyes on this Valentine's Day, her daughter's fifth birthday. *Oh, Toro, and just when I was starting to like you!*

✍

Six weeks later, I packed up my house to head back to California, not to return for ten months. I'd already said goodbye to Felipe, Jessica, Daniel, and Veronica, hugging them tight and promising to bring them presents on my next trip to La Perlita in January.

"I want Barbie clothes," Jessica said, her dark eyes sparkling in anticipation.

"I want a remote control car," Felipe said.

"Me, too, a black one," Daniel chimed in, flashing his nine-year-old boyish grin.

"And you, Veronica?"

"I'd like a backpack and some school supplies, Rebecca, if that's okay."

"Of course it's okay. You all be good while I'm gone. No scaling the wall and jumping in the pool. Felipe? Daniel? You promise?"

"We promise," the boys said, but neither quite looked me in the eye. Like it or not, I knew they might not keep their promise. A cool swimming pool in the upcoming hot, humid months would be a temptation, especially since the boys were agile enough to climb the wall.

"If I get word from the gardener or the maintenance guy that you've been in the pool, no presents. Deal?"

"Oh…okay," Felipe said.

The next morning, sitting outside on the curb, I said goodbye to Toro. A strong, balmy wind mussed my hair. "I haven't heard yelling or crying for a while. Everything okay with Felipe?"

"He's better. Not good, but better."

"Have you found any alone time with him?"

"I've taken him over to the new house I'm building—to check on the workers. He's helped carry bricks for the masons."

"Good start. Well, I'm leaving tomorrow. I want to be home for Easter."

"That's what the kids told me. You're back in November, correct?"

"Usually, but this year I'm going to spend Thanksgiving and Christmas with my family. While I'm gone, I give you full permission to party every night. Make as much noise as you want and let off firecrackers to your heart's delight," I said, and laughed.

"Thanks for that *permiso*," Toro replied, with a slight smile.

"And, remember, if you can hear the church bombs go off on Easter Sunday you need to go to church."

"What?" he asked, looking confused.

"It's a joke I tell my friends. Only sinners can hear the church bombs."

Toro didn't laugh, so I continued, "Anyway, would you watch my house while I'm gone? Make sure the kids that walk this way into town don't paint graffiti on my outside wall, and that nobody, including Felipe and Daniel, climb the wall into my yard?"

"I can do that."

"Gracias," I said.

Toro stood, and we hugged. Actually, he stood still. I hugged.

❧CHAPTER TWENTY-THREE❧

March, 2011 - California

Back in California the following day, I sat down for dinner with Jason, a retired football coach, and my boyfriend of many years.

"What's going on with your new neighbors?" he asked, pouring us each a glass of wine.

He toasted my return, and I smiled, glad to be home for a spell. "Felipe is a handful. He keeps acting out at school. I've threatened to go to school with him and sit in his classroom until he learns to behave."

Jason burst out laughing, remembering how I had done exactly that to my daughter Summer when she was in eighth grade. After receiving notes from Summer's teachers and calls from the school principal about her joking around in class and falling grades, I'd decided to attend school with her.

"Mom, please!" Summer implored. "Don't embarrass me."

"Summer, I'm leaving work anyway because of you. I might as well stay a while."

"Mom!"

"Summer. I'll attend your classes for as long as you need me to. When you straighten up, I'll stop going. It's up to you."

The memory of her friends calling out between classes, "Summer, your mom's here," still makes me laugh, six years later.

Jason passed me the plate of garlic-seasoned potatoes. "How's Jessica?"

"She's a delight. I love her like a granddaughter. She draws me pictures almost every day—pictures of her with long black hair and me with my red curly hair. She depicts us holding hands and adds in lots of red and pink hearts. Her drawings are taped to my refrigerator door."

"I get your love for the kids," Jason said. "And especially little Jessica...she's such a doll. But, I don't like your friendship with their father."

"I wouldn't say we're 'friends' yet, but I don't fear him as much as before. I think we can become friends. Eventually. Maybe."

"You're flirting with danger, Rebecca. Why do you even want to cozy up to that guy? What's the attraction?"

"I told you, God told me to love him."

"Well, I don't understand that kind of love. And from what you've told me, he's a bad guy. A loser."

"So only 'good' people deserve love, Jason? When should I give up on somebody? Is there a scale of 'badness'...where we stop caring about another human being?"

"Didn't someone you know in La Perlita tell you last year that your new 'buddy' Toro is suspected of killing three people for not paying their debts? And he buried them out in the jungle?"

"Yes."

"That doesn't scare you, Rebecca? You don't stop to think you're involved in a precarious friendship?"

I sat up straight to defend Toro, for some reason I didn't understand. "It's a rumor. There's no proof. You know how people talk and speculate."

"Where's there's smoke, expect to find fire," Jason said, raising his husky voice a notch.

Sipping the cool wine, I looked out the glass patio doors, ignoring Jason's irritation. Spring rain fell gently on the grass and flowers in the backyard. "Everybody deserves a chance to change," I finally said. "I see good in him."

"Like what? What good can you possible see in a lowlife who sells drugs for a living—and probably kills people?"

I thought for a moment. "He loves his children...in his own way. He goes to school when Felipe gets in trouble. He doesn't have to do that. He acknowledges and provides for Marco when he could have just abandoned him..."

My mind raced to come up with more examples of "good." "Nelly told me he paid to keep his brothers in school when his father wanted to pull them out years ago. He sponsors a Barrio soccer team, and I've heard he keeps petty crime in hand."

"Well, I'm not all spiritual like you and I see the devil. A real lost cause. Give it up. Who gave you the job to save all the bad guys in the world?"

"I'm not stupid or ignorant of danger. I just care for those who God sets down in front of me. The ones I feel led to reach. I know it's hard to understand, Jason. It's not my love. It's His." *I wish Jason was more of a believer in Christian ideals. Life would be easier.*

"I don't get what you're trying to prove. You keep this up and you'll get yourself killed."

I stopped for a moment to look at Jason—dark, handsome, opinionated, and always concerned about me. "Who's going to kill me? Toro likes me...I think."

I understood Jason's concern. And I loved him for caring. *But, if I allow my mind to entertain all the negative things about Toro— imagined or maybe real—fear will suffocate me. So I choose to think positive thoughts.*

❧

The magic of technology—Internet, Facebook, Messenger— bridged my life in the U.S. with life in La Perlita during the months I was away. I routinely exchanged texts with Cesar, my friend and handyman; Francisco, the gardener; Ramon, the pool cleaner; and a multitude of friends. News was just a keyboard stroke away.

A week after my return to California, Nelly accepted my Facebook "friend request."

Hola, Nelly. How are you?

Bien, Rebecca, gracias.

How are Felipe and Jessica?

They're good.

Is Felipe behaving at school?

Sometimes.

I'll help you with that when I return, if you want.

Yes. Gracias.

Tell the kids I send hugs and say hi to Toro for me.

I will.

⌘CHAPTER TWENTY-FOUR⌘

January, 2012 - La Perlita

I returned to La Perlita after ten months of golfing, visiting friends, church activities, and celebrating Christmas and New Year's with family. I left pristine neighborhoods with their manicured lawns, traffic lights, busy freeways, and well-stocked supermarkets for the simple, slow-paced life in the tropics.

My sister, Tina met me at the Puerto Vallarta airport to drive me into La Perlita. "Good to see you, Sis," I said. "Did you miss me? Are those new glasses? I like your short haircut. How is Joaquin? How's the town?"

Tina laughed. "Slow down. I can't answer that fast. And why do you always have so much luggage?"

"Because during the off season I find all kinds of things I can't live without down here."

"Like what?" she asked.

"Well...like the aluminum geckos that will look spectacular on the wall near the pool, a flat screen TV, air mattresses..." I continued through the sundry of items I had packed away in my luggage, while Tina shook her head in amusement.

Ten years older, Tina was the reason I lived in La Perlita. She and her ex-husband, Bill brought me to this fishing village with them on vacation when I was seventeen. Now Tina lived here full-time, and I wintered here.

We settled in for the thirty-minute trip to my house. The minutes flew by as we chatted non-stop. The town was recuperating from a stormy rainy season, Tina reported. Joaquin was good except for his arthritic knees, her three adult children had spent Christmas with her, and she had no local gossip to share.

"You know you're the one who knows everything going on— even when you're away," Tina said, tucking her left foot up onto the seat, operating the brake and gas pedals with her right. "Joaquin says he can't wait to see you so you can fill him in on what's happening in his own town."

I laughed. "Well, tell him to give me at least forty-eight hours before I'll have all the latest news."

The sight of palm trees and banana orchards settled over me like a calming balm. I opened the car window to feel the warm breeze. Light humidity. Tropics. "I love being here," I told my sister. "I love the weather, the palm trees, and gorgeous orange and red sunsets. The margaritas."

"Me too. Besides the ocean and great weather, I like the friendliness of the people and the slow pace of life. I don't miss the U.S. much at all."

"I like the States and my family too much to live here *all* the time," I said.

"How was your holiday?" she asked.

"I had a great time. I enjoy spending Christmas with Jason and my kids. And the grandbabies make it extra special. The cold and rainy weather I can live without though. It feels refreshing — once in a while. Quite different from Christmas on the beach."

Tina chuckled. "Did you stay in the States this year for the holidays to be with your family or to be away from Toro and all the noise in your neighborhood?"

"Both," I replied honestly, content to be back in La Perlita. "What do you think Toro has in store for me this season?"

"Hopefully nothing you can't handle, Sis," Tina said.

⁋

Tina drove down the main road into town. I was ecstatic to see the deep blue waters of the Pacific Ocean on my right and palm trees on the left. Home.

Felipe and Jessica saw me in Tina's car as we passed by their house. They ran alongside the vehicle as Tina rounded the corner.

"Rebecca!" they yelled in unison as I opened the passenger-side door.

"*Hola.* How are you?" I asked, hugging them both.

"I missed you so much, Rebecca," Jessica said, her wide bright eyes gleaming in delight. "Tomorrow is *Dia de Reyes.*"

I nodded and smiled; glad I had arrived prepared with presents for Felipe, Jessica, Veronica, and Daniel for Three Kings Day. The holiday represents the height of the Christmas season, and commemorates the three wise men who had traveled from afar, bearing gifts for baby Jesus.

Through experience, I knew the children in La Perlita, and throughout Latin America, look forward to this day, like Christmas morning in the States.

I was ready.

"Well, I guess you'll have to wait until tomorrow to see if The Kings bring you presents. Were you good this year?"

"*¡Sí!*" Jessica squealed.

"Felipe?"

"Mostly," he said, giving me an impish grin.

⋘

A few minutes later, Felipe and Jessica struggled to roll my suitcases through the patio door.

"They're heavy. Be careful," I called out.

I gave my sister a big hug. "Thanks for the ride, Sis. I'll unpack and meet you at your house in two hours. The sunset and a strawberry margarita are calling my name. You in?"

"You bet."

"Rebecca, can we help you unpack?" Felipe asked, most likely wanting to see if I had presents in my suitcases.

"No, but thank you for asking," I replied, eager to reunite with my home and settle in.

"Are you sure?" Jessica asked, stalling.

"I'm sure...but let's sit a minute, put our feet in the pool, and you can tell me what you've been up to."

"Okay," they said, throwing off their sandals and running to the pool steps.

Jessica sat close to my side and held my hand. "Felipe got suspended from school, Rebecca," she said, innocently.

"Felipe?"

"It wasn't my fault. A fifth-grader, Juan, always picks on me. I got angry and punched him." He pouted, making small waves with his hand in the pool.

"Why does he pick on you?" I asked.

Felipe stalled. "He...he...says my dad is a bad man."

"Oh, Felipe. I'm sorry. Did you tell your mom or dad this?"

"No."

"Did you tell a teacher?"

"No."

"My daddy isn't a bad man, Rebecca...is he?" Jessica asked.

I gathered both children in my arms. "Your daddy loves both of you. That's what's important. Kids say mean things. But fighting isn't the answer, Felipe."

"I wrote you letters all the time," Jessica said.

"You did? Where did you send them?"

"They're in the mail box by your door."

"Oh, thank you, sweetie. I'll read them. Now I have to go. Tina is waiting for me in town."

With sad faces, Felipe and Jessica hugged me and made their way to the door.

"I'll see you tomorrow. I promise," I called after them.

Minutes later, I exchanged my long pants and sweater for cool summer clothes. After emptying the suitcases, I plugged in the charger to my new electric bike and set up my laptop in the upstairs office. *Enough for now.*

"*Hola*, Tony. It's Rebecca," I spoke into the house phone. "Can you take me into Tina's?"

"Sure. I'll be right there. *Bienvenida!*"

Tony had lived in La Perlita all sixty years of his life and knew everybody and everything that went on within a fifty-mile radius. He had an opinion about all of it, which he would share...if he trusted you as a friend. It was like driving around with a monthly journal magazine. Tony and I routinely figured out solutions to the world's problems during our rides between my house in the Barrio and downtown La Perlita—ten minutes away.

Tony always took the same route. He passed Toro's, then Gloria's one-bedroom brick house, and then turned west onto the main street through the Barrio. I waved to Manuel at the small corner market, to Maria Jose at the tortilla factory, and Alberto at the Internet Café. A block later, Tony turned into the subdivision to avoid the speed bumps on every corner through the Barrio.

"What's up with the cartels?" I asked after a few pleasantries. "The U.S. media acts like all of Mexico is dangerous. Friends up north can't believe I feel safe here."

"We're feeling the effects of that fear," Tony said. "If it weren't for the Canadians, who are not subject to the scare tactics you have in the United States, we wouldn't have any tourists."

I heard the frustration in his voice.

"I'm sorry for you and all the locals who depend on tourist money, Tony. But when we see severed heads, and bodies hanging from bridges, along with reports of massive shootings, kidnappings and torture, it's hard to book a vacation into the middle of that."

"It's true those things happen. But not everywhere. Not here. And yet all of Mexico is impacted," he said, stopping in front of Tina's place.

I paid the two-dollar fare. "I agree it's not fair. We'll talk more later. Okay?"

"Sure. And Rebecca, welcome back. We missed you."

"*Gracias*, Tony. Say hello to your wife."

❧CHAPTER TWENTY-FIVE❦

The following morning, I rode my electric bike past Toro's house and found it and the beer store closed. *Looks like Toro and Nelly are observing Three Kings Day. Nice.*

Not bothering to stop, I continued the fifteen-minute bike ride into town, traveling out of the Barrio and through El Tropical subdivision. I peddled passed the medical clinic and out onto the main cobblestone street heading into La Perlita. My heart soared and the smile on my face widened each time someone called out, *"Hola, Rebecca. Bienvenida!"*

I responded and waved at the women sweeping the sidewalk in front of their homes, to the taxi drivers passing by in their yellow cabs, to restaurant owners decorating plastic tables with bright colored tablecloths, and to street vendors preparing their sales of necklaces, bracelets, and wood sculptures. *How can I not love it here?*

I stopped first at Chato and Marta's house. *"Hola, familia,"* I called out, walking into their spacious home. "Don't you guys ever lock the door?"

"Welcome back, Rebecca. It's about time you returned," Chato said.

"Hi, Marta," I said, embracing her.

"What's going on, Chato? Why are you in a wheelchair?" I asked, crossing the dark-brown floor tiles to plant a kiss on his cheek. "I wasn't gone *that* long, was I?"

Chato smiled, but I noticed sadness in his light brown eyes. "Diabetes," he said.

"*Oh, mi amigo.* That's not good. Is it all the churros? Or is it the tequila?" I asked, teasing him.

"It's the churros, and cake, and donuts," Marta said, with a chastising look at her husband. "I'm trying to limit his sugars. I don't want to lose him."

"The good living has come back to bite me," he replied, patting his large stomach. "I have nerve-ending problems. I forget what the doctors call it. But it hurts to stand or walk."

"Neuropathy?" I asked.

"Something like that," he replied. "But enough about me. I'm growing old. What have you been doing that you stayed away so long?"

"Family," I answered. "You know how torn I am between life here and life in California."

I settled into the thick-cushioned chair Marta placed next to Chato in their living room and reached out to hold his hand. "*Amigo*...you have to take care of yourself. You can't grow old on me...I need you. Marta needs you."

"I'm not going anywhere...or if I am, I'll go slow. I promise," he said cheerfully.

"I'm holding you to that, amigo."

Chato and I sat together for a moment, sharing memories of the late '60s when we'd danced all night at La Perlita's Sunset Bar, right on the beach. *Where had the years gone?*

"I've been glued to the news and internet for months following this Mexican drug war," I told Chato. "I never used to care as much, but knowing Toro is somehow involved makes it seem so real to me."

"That's understandable. Last year was violent for Mexico," Chato said. "La Perlita isn't directly affected, but the drug war is all over the news. Ever since President Calderon took office six years ago and set out to eliminate the cartels, it's become worse. All of us are implicated one way or another—just for being Mexicans."

Marta returned from the adjoining kitchen, offering coffee. "Over the past five years, nearly 48,000 people have been killed in drug-related violence," she said, sitting next to me. "Each year it's worse. And that's not counting the thousands of people who've gone missing."

"I heard those numbers, too," I said. "But you guys don't even lock your doors. Aren't you afraid for your own lives?"

"No, those deaths are mainly cartel against cartel, like happens in the United States when gangs set out to eliminate each other and take over new territory," Chato said.

"Why, Chato? Why such violence down here?" I asked my dear friend.

"Money," he said. "Because Mexican traffickers control the flow of most of the cocaine, heroin, foreign-produced marijuana, and meth into the United States. That's billions of dollars. They're killing each other to take over supply routes."

I set my coffee on the side table. "With billions flowing around, I see why there's enough money to bribe authorities."

"It's a combination of threats and money. The gangsters offer a police officer or city official *'plata o plomo,'*" Chato informed me.

"What does that mean, 'plata o plomo'?"

"It's a phrase in Spanish for 'silver or lead.' meaning, 'accept a bribe or face assassination,'" he explained.

What a difficult, complex situation. "Even so, I understand the Mexican military are fighting against the organized crime families," I said. "Isn't it true that several cartel leaders were recently arrested and extradited to the United States, and police officers, including a police chief, were arrested on charges of protecting Los Zetas cartel?"

"That is true," Marta said. "But they kill or arrest one leader and there's three more to take his place. It seems never-ending."

Chato smiled. "You've done your homework on this, amiga."

"It's because of my concern for Toro and his family," I said. "And, because my fellow Americans like to talk about 'them damn Mexicans' and their drug cartels. Yet, when you look below the surface, it's we *gringos* who are mostly at fault—for wanting the drugs in the first place and for supplying most of the guns for the killings."

Chato laughed. "You're a redhead with green eyes and freckles, yet you defend Mexico and speak Spanish fluently...you're really one of us," he said.

His words touched my heart. "Gracias, amigo. But no, I'm definitely an American and love my country. I just don't like the way the media portrays Mexico. That's the 'defender' in me."

I patted Chato's hand. "By the way, I read that La Familia cartel has finally been exterminated. It's weird your government used that word 'exterminated'—like they're bugs or something. They say the new dominant force in Michoacán and Jalisco is The Knights Templar. Is that what you've heard?"

"Yes," Marta said. "They're called Los Templarios and they're a splinter group of La Familia now fighting *against* La Familia. That may not be good for Toro. He's aligned with La Familia."

"What could happen?" I asked, startled.

"We don't know," Chato replied. "This is all new for us. We're hoping this organized crime inbreeding and infighting stays far away from La Perlita."

I rose to leave. "Well, I'm sorry to raise cartel news and then run, but I came into town for groceries and need to get back. I have presents for Toro and Nelly's kids and Nelly's younger siblings for Three Kings Day."

"Stop by again soon...and bring Tina," Marta said. "We haven't seen your sister for months."

"I will. Love you guys. Adios!"

꿏

Late that afternoon, as I finished setting up the house and stocking the refrigerator, the doorbell rang repeatedly, signaling the arrival of the kids. "I'll be right there," I said, looking down from the balcony.

Veronica, Daniel, Felipe, and Jessica rushed in as I opened the patio door.

"Happy Dia de Reyes," I said, hugging each one, delighted to see them. "Are you here to see me, or to see if The Kings left presents somewhere around here for you?"

"Both!" they yelled in unison.

I motioned to the outside table and chairs. "Okay. Well sit down and I'll go inside to see if I can find anything."

The kids ran to obey, vying for their favorite chairs.

"Look at this. There are presents here," I said moments later feigning surprise.

One by one they opened their gift bags.

"Thank you for the remote control helicopter," Daniel said. "I love it."

"Wow, I got a remote control car. Thank you, Rebecca."

The delight in the two boy's eyes warmed my heart.

"Just what I wanted," Jessica exclaimed. "A new Barbie. And, what's this, Rebecca?" she asked, holding up a square box.

"Open it and see."

"I'll help you, Jessica," Felipe said. Together they opened the bright-colored box to find a Barbie tent.

"Let's set it up," Daniel offered.

Within minutes, Jessica and her Barbie doll sat inside her new three-foot-high pop-up tent with Barbie's colorful image on all sides. "I love it, Rebecca. Gracias."

Veronica watched Jessica playing inside her Barbie tent and smiled as she sorted through her school supplies. She placed them inside her new Selena Gomez backpack. "Gracias, Rebecca," she said with a big smile.

"You're welcome, Veronica. How is school?"

"It's good. I'm getting all 10's."

"Wonderful. That's the same as all A's in the United States. Do you have a career goal?"

"Yes. I want to be a pastry chef."

I held Veronica close and tucked stray bangs behind her right ear. "I'm proud of you."

⊷

The following day, I stopped by the beer store. "Hola, Nelly."

"Hola, Rebecca. Thank you for the gifts for the kids. You spoil them. You're way too nice."

"It's okay. I love bringing presents. Years ago, I adopted your siblings, and now your children."

Nelly nodded and flashed me one of her friendly smiles, highlighted by dimples. "The kids miss you when you're gone. I spend the entire off-season telling them how many months, weeks, and days before you'll be back."

"Is it the presents they're waiting for?" I asked with a laugh.

"That's probably a part of it...but I think it's because you give them so much attention. They feel safe with you."

How intuitive for a twenty-three-year-old. "It's good to know they care," I said softly.

"Even little Marco has been looking for you."

"Marco?"

"Toro's son. He must remember being in your pool last season. Once he learned to walk on his own, and the kids or I took our eyes off of him—we'd find him at your door, knocking."

"Oh, geez. He must walk fast."

"He does. He's almost two."

"Well, I look forward to seeing him. Is Toro around? I wanted to say hi."

"No. He, Julio and Miguel went up the coast on business."

"They have beer business up the coast? Don't the Corona trucks deliver to them here?" I asked, playing naïve.

"Yes. But, they're looking for a better distributor. Better prices or something," she said, looking down at the counter.

"Okay. While I'm here, I wanted to talk about Felipe. He'll be returning to school next week, right?"

"Yes."

"He told me he's gotten into some trouble."

Nelly sighed and shook her head. "Yes, we get called in to school at least once a week. His teacher says he's not listening, or he doesn't turn in homework, or he's being the class clown. It's frustrating."

"Would you like me to help?" I asked.

"Yes. I would."

"Okay. Good. When can we go to the school and talk to the teacher? Maybe we can come up with a plan of action."

"How about Thursday morning, seven thirty?" Nelly asked. "I'll set it up. That'll give us time to talk to his teacher before school starts at eight. Meet me here and I'll drive us over."

I smiled, glad to see baby steps of progress. "That works fine."

As I walked back to my house, I wondered if this was a good thing—getting so involved in Felipe's problems at school. *How can I not? This is who I am and what I do...helping people resolve problems. And I love Felipe.*

❧CHAPTER TWENTY-SIX❧

At seven thirty on Thursday morning, I stepped up into the passenger seat of Nelly's Chevy SUV. Jessica and Felipe, dressed in their blue and white school uniforms, settled into the back seat.

"You're going to school with us?" Jessica asked, excitement in her voice.

"For a few minutes, sweetie," I said. "To meet Felipe's teacher." I noticed Felipe staring blankly out his window.

"Is Felipe in trouble again, Rebecca?" Jessica wanted to know.

"No, honey. I just want to meet his teacher."

"Felipe, what's your teacher's name?" I asked to engage him in conversation.

"*Maestro* Julio."

"Is he nice?" I asked.

"No."

I looked at Nelly, who raised her eyebrows but stayed silent as we turned the corner, heading to the school.

Where do we go with that indictment? I wondered.

Jessica filled the silence as if the world rotated around her. "I'm reading a book about a little girl and her pet crocodile," she said.

"A crocodile?" I asked.

"Yes. Her name is Croaky."

"Whose name is Croaky?" her mother wanted to know. "The crocodile or the little girl?"

"The crocodile," Jessica squealed and giggled.

My heart ached for Felipe, who remained sullen and tense, staring out the window as his little sister chatted on.

The elementary school was located halfway into La Perlita, a mile from my and Nelly's houses, on a dusty road with potholes that got bigger each year. We passed dozens of women with babies in strollers and young children in school uniforms, walking to school—those living close enough to walk, or those not fortunate enough to own a vehicle or possibly not having extra pesos to take the local bus.

Nelly parked in front of the red-bricked school next to the eight-foot-high chain link fence that kept the students in and others out. Nelly explained our appointment with *Maestro* Julio, and the teacher at the gate allowed us to enter.

Jessica hugged her mom and me and ran off to play hopscotch with a friend while Felipe remained at my side. I bent down and whispered in his ear. "It'll be okay. You're not in trouble."

"I get a whipping every time my parents come to school because of me," he whispered back, his small face full of worry.

"Well, not today. This is a good visit...not a 'you're-in-trouble' visit." I reached for his hand, but he pulled it away. Obviously holding an almost-nine-year-old's hand in public was universally unacceptable.

The three of us crossed a combination dirt and cement playground. The one-story school, built in an L-shape, housed eighteen classrooms plus an office. Nelly explained there were three classrooms for each grade, with an average of twenty-six students per classroom. I did the math...four hundred and eight students between the ages of six and twelve. *Lots of elementary age children for this village of five thousand.*

Felipe's teacher, Julio, tall with dark hair and glasses, invited us into the vacant classroom. Nelly and I squeezed into the student desks with attached chairs at the front of the class, nearest the teacher's desk. Felipe sat in the desk next to his mom.

"How can I help you?" the teacher asked, looking at Nelly.

Nelly deflected the question to me. "*Hola*, Maestro Julio. My name is Rebecca. I'm Felipe's neighbor and a family friend."

He stared at me, a questioning frown in his forehead. "How can I help *you*?"

"I understand Felipe is struggling in your class and school in general. I'd like to be of assistance," I replied, looking fondly at Felipe, who stared at the desktop.

"How so?" he asked.

"I'm willing to tutor Felipe and I'm even willing to attend classes with him."

"Attend classes with him?" he asked, surprised. "That's highly irregular."

"Maybe so, but it can be effective if Felipe is having difficulties staying in his desk or paying attention."

Nelly nodded in agreement.

Felipe's teacher looked at Felipe, then Nelly and then back to me. "Felipe doesn't need a babysitter, *Señora*. This is third grade. Felipe needs to stay in his seat, complete his schoolwork, listen and obey. So...Thank you for the offer, but no thanks."

Seriously? You're refusing help? I wanted to shout.

"Anything else?" he asked, obviously cutting the visit short.

Nelly glanced at me and shrugged her shoulders as if to say, "Sorry."

"Yes," I replied. "If you'd be willing to prepare a list of missing assignments and provide the work books, I'll help Felipe catch up."

"I can do that," his teacher said, starting to rise from his desk.

"And," I continued, "is there extra work Felipe can complete to raise his grade?"

Maestro Julio sat back down and looked at a ledger on his desk. "We're just starting the second half of this year. Felipe has an average of six in our grading system. I believe that's a C-minus in U.S. terms."

I nodded the affirmative.

"If he completes the packets I'll provide you, Señora Rivera," he continued, looking at Nelly, "he can raise his grade to a C-plus or B-minus. If he does well on the assignments and tests, no extra work is needed."

"Thanks for your time, Maestro," Nelly said, wiggling out of the desk.

As Felipe and Nelly made their way through the classroom door, I stayed behind. "May I speak to you in confidence?" I asked.

"Yes. What is it?"

"Felipe tells me he's being bullied by a fifth grader, by the name of Juan," I informed him. "Did you know this?"

Maestro Julio shook his head.

"He says kids tell him his father is a bad man. As you know, he's starting to fight back."

The teacher hesitated a moment. "I'll be honest, Señora. I'm from Guadalajara, but I've heard Felipe's father has a reputation in this town. It's not surprising students hear things at home from their parents and take it out on Felipe."

He paused again. "I'm wondering how you came to be a family friend. Is that wise?"

I had heard this question from others. "Children should not have to pay for the sins of their fathers," I replied, irritation edging into my usually calm voice.

I took a deep breath to steady my voice. "I've heard the stories from locals about his early childhood. Did you know he attended this school? He loved school and wanted to be a professional soccer player. His father crushed those dreams when he pulled Toro out in the fifth grade...to work. Given your educational level, it's obvious that didn't happen to you...or me. We had options he didn't."

I looked outside and saw Nelly waiting patiently under the big tree in middle of the schoolyard. "He went on to make terrible choices. And with those choices come consequences. I'm not sure about you, *Maestro*, but I don't think Felipe should pay for that."

Felipe's teacher stared at me and I wondered if I'd been too forthcoming. Then I saw a flash of understanding in his eyes.

"I love this family. I can't explain why," I said. "It goes against reason and the advice from my friends and family. So would you please look out for Felipe? I can handle the academic part—but if I can't be here at school with him, then I need you and others to protect him from bullies. Please?"

He nodded. "I'm willing to do that. Thank you for coming in today, Señora Rebecca."

"Thank you for your time, Maestro." I handed him a card with my house phone number. "Please call me at any time."

The teacher shook my hand. "Gracias."

Nelly and I drove home, setting up a homework schedule for Felipe. I wondered if Maestro Julio would keep his word and look out for Felipe, or if he considered him a lost cause.

❧

Toro stopped me as I walked to the corner store later that afternoon. "Gracias," he said.

"For what?"

"For going to Felipe's school today. You didn't need to do that."

"I wanted to. Felipe's a good kid. If he starts failing in school, he'll hate going. If he hates going, he'll make life miserable for himself and everybody."

"Why do you care?"

"I just do," I said. "I'm hoping if Felipe realizes people care, he'll make more of an effort."

"I hope so. My brothers and I never misbehaved in school like he does."

"Me either. But does the yelling, spanking, and grounding work?"

Toro half smiled. "It does for a day or two."

⮞CHAPTER TWENTY-SEVEN⮜

March 2012

"Sis, have you heard?" Tina asked when I answered her phone call in early March. "A Canadian man is missing. He's this guy everyone calls 'Tequila Joe.'"

Coffee and phone in hand, I moved to the balcony to enjoy the morning sun. A herd of cows grazed in a nearby field. "Missing where? And what kind of name is Tequila Joe?" I asked, curious and unconcerned.

"It's his nickname...obviously he loves Tequila," Tina said.

"Do you know him?" I asked.

"I've seen him and his dog around town for years during the high season. Joaquin just told me somebody may have kidnapped him."

I set my coffee on a side table. My curiosity turned to shock. "What? Kidnapped? Why is kidnapping even a rumor? That doesn't happen here!"

"I'm just telling you what someone told Joaquin this morning," Tina said.

I heard the alarm in my sister's voice. "Okay. Let me check it out, Sis. I'll call you back."

๛

An hour later, after speaking with the mayor and police chief, I called Tina. "Here's what I've learned so far. He was drinking with friends at Lupe's Bar two nights ago. A friend from Villa Caliente asked for a ride home. The friend says they stopped first at the ATM outside the Bancomer Bank, and then Tequila Joe dropped him off at his house. He hasn't been seen since."

"What about his jeep and dog?" Tina asked.

"The authorities didn't mention a jeep or a dog."

"He has a small, white-haired mutt that went everywhere with him. And he drives an older, black jeep," my sister said.

I shook my head in disbelief. "Well, a jeep and dog weren't reported as found, so I'd say Tequila Joe, the dog, *and* his jeep are all missing.

"That's so sad," Tina said. "You don't think Toro knows anything, do you?"

"I can't imagine why. But let me check," I promised.

I approached Toro napping in his hammock. "Good morning," I said, swinging the hammock back and forth to wake him up.

"What's up?" he asked, squinting into the morning sun.

"There's a Canadian man missing. Have you heard anything?"

"I don't hang with Canadians or gringos," he said, gruffly and closed his eyes.

"Well, he drove into Villa Caliente to take a friend home two nights ago and hasn't been seen since. His friends are worried."

"I'll let you know if I hear anything," he muttered.

So much for my information gathering.

⤎

By the end of the day, the news of a long-time seasonal visitor to La Perlita gone missing was ablaze around town. He'd often bought pot. Everyone speculated—was it drug related? He had a temper when he drank too much. Had he gotten into a fight? He had a girlfriend. Was there another woman involved? Had he left for a while without telling anybody?

Within days, a newspaper in Joe's hometown in Canada ran the story about one of their own missing in Mexico.

A palpable sense of fear clouded the normal "we're in paradise" atmosphere. I no longer walked home alone after dark. The taxi drivers stayed outside my house until I was safe inside.

"I hate this feeling, Tony," I complained a week after Tequila Joe's disappearance. "I used to say the only dangerous things in La Perlita were the uneven sidewalks."

Tony laughed. "That's still mostly true," he said.

"Home invasions, kidnappings, murders, robberies, and stuff happen every day in California, and I've stopped paying much attention over the years. But one thing happens here, and it's devastating," I said, preparing to open the taxi door.

"I think it's because we're such a small town," he said. "That brings it closer to home."

Tony accepted the pesos from my hand. "Toro doesn't scare you?" he asked.

"He used to. Not anymore. We have a strange relationship I can't even describe. I do get nervous at times when I think about who he *may* be and how others describe him as so dangerous. My boyfriend Jason calls it a 'precarious friendship.' I call it a 'precarious endeavor.'"

I hesitated a moment, reflecting on my feelings. "But, I'm strangely not afraid of him anymore. Well...maybe a little. I get scared when I read what other *narco traficantes* have done. The tortures. The murders. I might be wrong, but I don't see that evil in Toro."

"Given his power in this town, he's not a bad friend to have, Rebecca. Just be careful. Don't get too close."

"I won't."

"By the way, what do you think happened to that Canadian?" Tony asked.

"I don't have a clue. I hope he took off somewhere and doesn't realize everybody's worried about him," I answered.

∽

A friend in the States heard about Tequila Joe's disappearance via social media and sent me quotes from U.S. Travel Warnings issued the previous month. "...An increasing number of innocent people are being targeted by transnational criminal organizations," it said, "something that Mexican President Felipe Calderón generally doesn't like to acknowledge or discuss. The number of Americans killed in Mexico rose to 120 in 2011."

I read the entire travel warning Online and saw that there were parts my friend had left out. I wrote back to him, sharing the additional information. "The Mexican government makes a considerable effort to protect U.S. citizens and other visitors to major tourist destinations." And, "There is no evidence that transnational criminal organizations have targeted U.S. visitors and residents based solely on their nationality."

Things were not as bleak as my friend believed them to be. And other reports had shown that the majority of the Americans killed in Mexico, were actually Mexican-Americans and somehow involved in the drug war.

⌒

Detectives out of San Sebastian worked the case, but two weeks passed and Tequila Joe was still missing. Town residents and visitors went about their daily business but fear and uncertainty hung in the air.

Then, a month after his disappearance, word hit the street. A farmer had found Tequila Joe tied to a tree in a nearby dense banana grove, not far off the main road into town. Dead.

The gnawing fear I had managed to block from my mind now invaded my heart and soul. Kidnapping and death. *This can't happen in a sleepy fishing village. It just can't!*

But it had. I was now afraid and angry. My paradise has been assailed by evil.

Hearing the news, I went straight to Toro's house. Nelly answered on my first knock.

"Good morning, Nelly. Is Toro home?" I asked quickly.

"No. He's over at Sandy's house."

I paused. "I'm sorry, Nelly. That must be so hard."

A glimpse of sadness appeared in Nelly's face, but her voice rang matter-of-fact. "He built a house for Sandy and Marco and stays with them three days a week. I deal with it. Nothing else I can do. Why do you need Toro?"

"Remember the Canadian who went missing a few weeks ago? He was found...dead...in a banana orchard."

"Yes, I know," she said, standing in her doorway. "The police talked to Toro yesterday. They showed him some pictures."

Did a drug related incident get Tequila Joe killed? I shuddered to entertain the thought.

"Why did the police talk to Toro?" I asked, curious as to Toro's involvement.

"They asked if he knew the guy and if he had any ideas on what happened."

Confused, I repeated my question. "Why Toro?" *Do they think he did this? Did they come to interrogate him?*

"He knows a lot about things around the area. I guess they figured he might know something about this."

"Did he?"

"No. Like Toro told the police. He doesn't know anything."

Toro arrived as Nelly and I talked. I waited to speak with him.

"Morning, Toro."

"What's up?" he asked.

Nelly gave him a quick not-so-friendly nod and went inside.

Toro and I sat down on the plastic chairs in front of his house.

"I just heard a farmer found Tequila Joe tied to a tree," I said.

"Yes," he responded.

"Nelly says the police came by here yesterday. Do they know what happened?" I asked.

Toro leaned back in his chair and placed his hands on his ever-expanding gut. "Only that he was bound by loose knots. They think maybe he died of a heart attack."

Tears sprung to my eyes. "That's so unfair," I finally said. "Who would have tied him to a tree? And why? That's just not right. I hear he was a great guy. He didn't deserve that. Nobody does."

I looked into Toro's face again for some emotion. *Did you do this?* I was smart enough to not ask.

"Doesn't make sense to me, either," he said. "I asked around. Nobody knows anything."

It couldn't have been Toro. I couldn't explain why, but I refused to believe he would do that. "This scares me," I said. "It makes me afraid to live out here in the Barrio all by myself, especially since I'm alone much of the time. I don't want to believe something so random can happen."

"Bad things happen everywhere, all the time," Toro said without inflection.

"I know...but I don't want it to happen *here*. I can't stop thinking about such a senseless act!"

Toro shrugged and shook his head.

A few moments later, Toro reached out and touched my hand. "You're not alone, you know. We're right here, *Gringa*." Taking a notebook out of his back pocket, he scribbled his number on a piece of paper and handed it to me. "Call if you need me."

207

Toro's words surprised and comforted me. "Really? Are you kidding? You'll be my bodyguard?" I asked, attempting humor to hide my feelings.

"Sure," he said with a slight smile.

"Okay, then. It's a deal. You're my bodyguard. Gracias."

We stood.

I began to walk away, but turned back, catching Toro's attention before he opened his front door. "Hey, Toro."

"*¿Sí?*"

"What's with this 'two women, two families, two houses'? Is this some kind of male fantasy you always wanted?" I smiled to take the edge off my sarcasm.

"Maybe. Or maybe it's taking responsibility and doing the right thing." With that, he opened the door and disappeared into the house.

His response surprised me and took the wind out of my righteous sail.

I walked away, hearing Jessica yell, "Papi!"

❧CHAPTER TWENTY-EIGHT❧

Two weeks later, Toro parked himself next to me on the curb as I looked over Veronica's English homework. "The police caught the guys that killed the Canadian," he said.

"I heard the same thing earlier today," I replied. "What exactly did *you* hear?"

"The police found the guy's jeep in Guadalajara. Evidence in the jeep led them back to a couple of thieves in Villa Caliente."

"And?"

"They've been arrested. They say they never meant to kill him. It was a robbery. They saw him get money from the ATM and followed. They forced their way into his jeep when he stopped somewhere."

"A robbery?" I asked, shaking my head in disbelief. "I heard different. That it was a mistaken identify. Somebody owning a black jeep owed money to some bad guys, and they killed Tequila Joe because he wouldn't hand the money over."

Toro stared at me for a moment. "My contacts in the police department say it was a robbery gone bad. The thieves said he was alive when they left him in the banana grove, and he could have untied himself."

I shook my head again and let out a deep breath. "Oh, geez. I don't know what to believe. But whatever it was, it's just sad."

"Did you know him?"

"No, but friends did, and they're crushed by his death. I'll let them know what you found out from the police—if they don't already know."

Toro stood to leave.

"Any word on a dog?" I asked.

"No."

⋘

Felipe grew accustomed to studying at my house after school three times a week for an hour. I struggled to keep his attention on schoolwork, however. Every five minutes he asked for a cup of juice, wandered to the balcony to look outside, or asked the time, wanting to ride his bike or play soccer in the park.

"Felipe. Concentrate, honey. Let's go over your arithmetic again."

His reward for completing homework and remaining caught up in class was to swim on Fridays. I remembered Toro telling me how Felipe would finish his homework but not turn it in, so I requested and received weekly reports from Maestro Julio. His grades improved although his in-class behavior continued to be problematic.

"Felipe, is that boy in fifth grade still bothering you?" I asked one afternoon.

"No, Rebecca. Not anymore."

"Very good." I wondered if Felipe suffered from attention deficit disorder, something not yet tested for in the poorly-resourced school.

❧

When the quarter progress reports came home, Toro stopped by. "Felipe's grades are better. Gracias," he said.

He showed me the report. Felipe had raised his average grade to a B-minus.

"My pleasure," I replied, standing in my patio doorway, amazed Toro had taken the time to stop by. "I'm glad his grades are improving. Now we have to keep on him."

We lingered in the doorway a moment watching a group of neighborhood children play in the park across the street. Orlando, a chubby ten-year-old, waved from Toro's tire swing.

I waved back. "Did you notice the For Sale sign at the edge of the park?" I asked.

"Yeah, but the guy's asking too much."

"Well, I hope nobody buys it," I said. "Without zoning laws in the Barrio anything could be built here...from a cantina to a boat storage facility, to an apartment complex."

Toro laughed, glancing at the piece of property. "I can't image an apartment complex there...but a cantina isn't a bad idea."

"Toro!" I punched him playfully in the shoulder. "No cantina. I prefer the kids have a place to play."

❧

In early April, two weeks after Toro's visit, my doorbell rang again and again.

Must be the kids. "Yes?" I said, looking over the balcony wall and down to the street.

Three little faces stared up at me—Felipe, Jessica, and Marco. "Which one of you can reach that doorbell?" I asked, surprised. My handyman, Cesar had purposely affixed the doorbell too high for smaller children to reach.

"Watch, Rebecca," Felipe said. He handed two-year-old Marco a stick and then picked him up by the waist. Marco reached high and pressed the doorbell with the stick. *Ding-dong, ding-dong.*

I laughed aloud. "Oh, my."

"We have a birthday invitation for you, Rebecca," Jessica said, shading her eyes with one hand, and showing me an envelope in the other.

"Whose birthday?" I asked, already knowing the answer.

"*Mio!*" squealed little Marco.

"Yours, Marco? Well, happy birthday! When's the party?"

"On Saturday," Felipe said. "Will you come?"

"I'll be there."

"Jessica and Marco want to know if we can swim today. Can we?" Felipe asked, hope written all over his face.

"Hmmm. Let me think. What do I have planned today?"

"Please, Rebecca," Jessica said, jumping up and down in place.

"Do you two have your homework done?"

"No...we're on Easter vacation, remember?" Felipe said, with a big smile.

"That's right," I replied, as if I'd forgotten. "Ask your mom and dad for permission. Then come by after lunch, get a trash bag and pick up the litter in the park and in the empty lot next door. Then you can swim."

"They already said we can swim today, Rebecca," Jessica said innocently.

"If it's all right with you," Felipe added with an impish grin.

"Then I'll see you after lunch."

"Veronica and Daniel want to come, too. And our cousins, Jorge, Teresa, and Jaime are at Grandma's house visiting. Can they come?" Felipe asked.

I did the math. Eight children. "Okay, but make that *three* big bags of trash. Clean from here, past your house, and up to the corner by the sports field."

"Thank you, Rebecca. And, can we have popcorn and some soda after we swim?"

"Soda, no. But popcorn and juice, yes. See you later."

Stepping back into my living room, I smiled to myself and thanked God for the neighborhood children. They made it easy to "love my neighbor."

$\approx$

Later that afternoon, after treating the kids to swimming and popcorn, I stopped to talk with Toro on our curb place.

"What's up Gringa," he asked as I sat down next to him, no longer sitting safely two feet away.

"The kids invited me to Marco's party," I said.

"You coming?"

"Yes. But I have a question."

"What question would that be?"

"Why are you having the party here? Does that mean Nelly is allowing Sandy on the street? From what Nelly told me a long time ago, Sandy's not allowed to even walk on this street, let alone show up here."

"That's still the way it is. But he's my son. There'll be a party."

"Without Sandy? You walk a fine line, amigo. It's amazing one of your two women hasn't kicked you to the curb."

Toro laughed aloud, and I joined him, knowing the audacity to speak my mind was still a novelty for him.

"We're having two parties. A small one at Sandy's and the big one here," he said, returning to his usual non-expressive mode.

"Well, only you could pull something like this off."

We sat by side for a few moments, neither one speaking.

I broke the silence. "So, should I expect noise, fireworks, and clowns?"

"Of course."

"I figured as much. Who's coming to this party?"

"Family and friends. My parents and my Uncle Juan are driving in from Michoacán."

"They're coming from eight hours away for a two-year-old's birthday party?" I asked surprised.

"That's how we do things here, Gringa," Toro said and smiled.

"Using any reason for a party?" I teased, enjoying the banter with my neighbor.

We sat comfortably in silence for a few more minutes. Toro suddenly asked, "What makes you do what you do?"

His question caught me off guard. "What do you mean?"

"You care about kids. You're part of the town-council and help raise money for town projects. I hear you helped that boy, Alberto, get a new wheelchair."

"The wheelchair idea was my friend, Cal's. I just helped make it happen."

After a few moments of measuring my words, I continued. "I used to be a mess, Toro. When I was younger...much younger...I used drugs and lived with a man who beat me. He put a contract on my life when I left him. I escaped and soon after contemplated suicide. I was so screwed up I didn't want to live."

Toro stared at me, with a look of disbelief.

"It's true. A group of Jesus people told me about God, new beginnings, and about salvation. Now...I'm different. Happy to be alive. Happy to help others."

Toro's gaze left my face. He stared at the ground. I felt him pull away and shut down.

"Toro?" I said, attempting to refocus his attention.

He stood and started to walk away. "I have to go. See you later."

Hmmm. I'd hoped sharing part of my checkered past might open up a deeper conversation. Guess not.

∾

Two days later, lively children's music blared over loud speakers, announcing Marco's birthday celebration.

I get much less annoyed attending these events then sitting at home resenting them, I thought, as I walked toward the party.

Passing "the macho-guy's-party table," as I now called the place Toro sat with a few select male guests drinking tequila shots, I noticed two new faces.

I picked the man on the left as Toro's father, since they looked similar with round faces, chipmunk cheeks, and thick black hair. Silver streaks throughout his father's hair provided a preview of Toro later in life.

The other man with his elbows on the table I took to be Toro's Uncle Juan. Heavy-set, looking to be in his early fifties, the man displayed muscled shoulders bunching beneath a clean white T-shirt.

All three men looked at me as I approached.

Feeling bold, I said, "*Hola*, Toro. I love you," and then walked calmly on by.

I heard the men choke, spitting out their tequila.

"*Te amo*, Toro," I heard one of them say, mimicking my greeting. Laughter erupted.

Toro must be red as a beet, I figured, not quite daring to glance over my shoulder. I spotted Nelly with Marco in her arms by her front door and hurried toward them.

"So, I assume the older man sitting on Toro's left is his father?" I asked, still reeling from my boldness.

"Yes, and his Uncle Juan is on the right," Nelly said, with a sweet smile.

"So, do you think I just embarrassed Toro?" I asked, concerned I may have crossed a dangerous line.

"Pretty much," Nelly answered. "You are one of few who can get away with that."

"With what?" I asked.

"Joking with him in front of others. But don't worry. He won't do you harm," she said and laughed.

I removed Marco from Nelly's arms. "I hope not."

"You're safe, Rebecca. He likes you."

Relieved, I smiled and turned my attention to Marco. "Happy birthday, little Mickey Mouse," I said, admiring Marco's black and red mini-tuxedo and black hat with mouse ears. I carefully kissed him on the cheek, not wanting to smudge the penciled-in mouse whiskers.

"This reminds me of Jessica's party last year," I said, looking around at the Mickey Mouse piñata and the red and black crepe paper décor. "You're very creative, Nelly."

"Gracias. Marco loves Mickey Mouse, so it let me reuse some of the decorations from Jessica's party."

"So...you're okay with this? Marco's celebration here?" I asked.

Nelly flashed me a smile that almost reached her gorgeous eyes.

"I make it work, Rebecca," she said. She remained silent for a few moments looking in Toro's direction. "But excuse me. I need to help my mother-in-law get the food out."

"Sure. Let me help." I hugged Marco, set him down to play with Jessica, and followed Nelly into the house.

The extravagant children's birthday party I now came to expect from Nelly and Toro lasted throughout the day and late into the night. After food, cake, and presents, but before the raucous drinking, mariachi band, and firecrackers, I prepared to leave.

"Why you leaving so early, Gringa?" Toro asked as I approached to say goodbye.

"I'm meeting a group of friends for dinner," I replied, looking through his obvious drunkenness to see if he was angry about the earlier teasing.

"Okay, then. Is it true you leave soon for *el norte*?" he asked, slurring his words.

"Yeah, in two days. I'll stop by when I'm sure you're sobered up—and say goodbye."

"Hey! I'm not drunk."

I shook my head, chuckling. "Good night, Toro."

With a crooked smile, Toro lifted his drink to me and returned his attention to his father and uncle.

I hugged Toro's mother and Nelly, waved goodbye to the other guests, and headed home.

ᢒCHAPTER TWENTY-NINEᢒ

April, 2012 - California

Back in California, I returned to my stateside activities of family, friends, church, line dancing, and golf.

"I don't get your attraction to Mexico," my girlfriend Patty said during a lunch date a few days after my return.

"What do you mean?" I asked.

"It's dangerous. Don't you watch the news?"

I laughed. "Why do you like San Francisco?"

"What does that mean?" she asked, surprise in her voice.

"Don't you watch the news?" I countered with a smile. "Based on FBI data, Oakland, right outside of San Francisco, is considered the second most dangerous city in the United States."

I took a bite of my salad and set down my fork. "Every country, every state, and even every city has safe areas and dangerous areas, Patty. Mexico is no different. I don't go where terrible things are happening. And, I choose not to lock myself inside a gated community and live in fear."

Patty shook her head. "You don't think you're adding risk to your life by living in Mexico?"

"No more than traveling into any big city on the public rail system, where robberies at gunpoint happen. Truth is, when it's my time to die, it's my time. Wherever that is destined to be. Life is too short to live in fear."

"I'll leave that adventurous spirit to you," Patty said. "I'm content to stay close to home."

"I respect that. Some of the cartels do have a moral compass though," I told my friend.

"Being part of a cartel and having a moral compass don't go hand-in-hand, Rebecca."

"Sure they do. In fact, just last month, members from the Knights Templar Cartel hung huge banners on major bridges in seven counties in the state of Guanajuato, Mexico. They pledged to not provoke any violent acts during Pope Benedict's visit. The banners read, 'The Knights Templar Cartel proclaim we will not partake in any warlike acts. We are not killers. Welcome, Pope.'"

"You're teasing," Patty said.

"No. I'm not. Look it up. That really happened."

⁓

On April 17, Jason turned up the television. "Rebecca, come here. Look what's on the news!"

I rushed into the living room. "What?"

"Listen."

"El Chapo Guzman and his Sinaloa Cartel are in the news again," the commentator said. "Sources close to the Mexican cartel leader report the fourteen dismembered bodies found in plastic bags in Nuevo Laredo, Mexico, today are a message from El Chapo to the leadership of Los Zetas."

I stared at the TV screen, displaying plastic bags of body parts.

Oh, geez.

"Nuevo Laredo shares a 230-mile stretch of the U.S.-Mexico border along the state of Texas," the reporter announced. "Sources say El Chapo plans to take over the drug sales, called *plazas*, at that border and every other border along the U.S.-Mexico line."

A banner, placed over a freeway overpass in Nuevo Laredo, flashed on the TV screen. "The dismembered bodies were placed below banners," said the reporter. "Apparently signed by El Chapo himself, stating Nuevo Laredo is his."

I translated the main message of the banner for Jason. "It says, 'This is how you stop dumbass people—by cutting up all those rats who steal and get by from kidnapping and killing innocent people. Signed, El Chapo.'"

Jason turned down the TV volume. "Doesn't that scare you?"

"Yes, things like that are horrible and they do strike fear inside me. But, as I told Patty at lunch the other day, I won't live in fear...and Nuevo Laredo is thousands of miles from La Perlita. El Chapo is saying he's going to take over the border *plazas*, which means selling zones. That's far, far away."

"Not far enough away for me," Jason said.

"I know. You and I are very different in our thinking about Mexico. You're not alone in your beliefs and I'm not alone in mine. Bottom line for me is I feel safe in La Perlita. In fact I've joined the town council of business owners and am helping them in fund-raising projects. It feels like home to me."

"I know, Rebecca. I'm glad you feel safe there. I'm not against sharing your precious village a few weeks a year, but that's my limit. As for Toro and his cartel connections, *that* makes me nervous. Face reality, darling. If he becomes a target for a rival gang, you, as his neighbor, are in the crosshairs."

⧼CHAPTER THIRTY⧽

November 2012 ~ La Perlita

The delightful sound of chirping birds woke me. Opening the curtains of the French doors, I breathed in the cool breeze, which fanned my face. Another beautiful day in paradise. No obligations today. No town council meetings, no event planning, no play dates with the kids...just my home and me.

I'd been back in La Perlita for two weeks, enjoying the warmth and the peaceful days.

The doorbell interrupted my thoughts.

Putting on a sundress, I headed for the door. "Who's there?"

"*Nosotros!*" chanted little voices.

Oh, no. Smiling, I opened the door. "Yes?"

"My mommy made bread pudding this morning, Rebecca. We brought you some," Jessica said, looking adorable in a pink dress and matching sandals.

I accepted the plate, smelling the rich aroma of the warm bread pudding. "Why, thank you. How nice. I'll have it with my morning coffee."

Four little faces smiled at me. *They're up to something.* "You're out early. It's not even nine o'clock," I said, looking into the fresh-washed faces of Felipe, Jessica, Daniel, and Veronica. I noticed Felipe and Daniel had used gel to spike their hair. *Cute.*

"It's Saturday," Veronica said, sweetly.

"Yes, it is Saturday," I replied.

"And we don't have school today," Daniel announced.

"Okay," I replied, waiting for the plan they had come up with that would most likely include me.

"There's a carnival in town this weekend," Veronica said, hope in her face. "Will you take us? Toro went somewhere and Nelly says she's too pregnant to go."

I laughed. *Nelly is six months pregnant and already playing the pregnant card.*

"*Por favor?*" the kids pleaded.

So much for chilling at home. *Do I really want to do this?* "Okay," I said. "But give me a couple of hours to eat breakfast and get ready. I'll be at your house at eleven. We'll walk into town. Okay?"

"Yes!" they chanted, giving me a hug before running back next door.

Sitting down to fresh bread pudding and coffee, I thought about the changes I'd witnessed since Toro moved in next door.

Two years ago, Toro wouldn't allow his children alone here at the house. He forbade me taking them anywhere. Now, they're here frequently and I'm allowed to take them into town. Maybe he's not worried about a rival gang kidnapping them, like Joaquin and Chato thought when we discussed this two years ago. Or maybe he trusts me to protect them? Or does he have people I'm not aware of—in the background—watching his kids and me when they're out of his sight? I had no answer to my musings and wasn't going to ask.

≪ଚ

A month later, Jason arrived for Christmas, bringing presents for all the kids—five of them now, including Marco. They were excited and grateful to receive toys, coloring books, and school supplies.

"Can we swim today?" Daniel asked, after opening gifts on Christmas afternoon.

I looked at Jason. "Sure," he said.

Marco left to spend the day with his mom, so four kids stayed to swim. Before the day ended, however, Ruben's three children—Teresa, Jorge, and Jaime—showed up for a surprise visit, adding to the noise and celebration.

"Daniel, Jaime, and Jorge need new clothes and shoes," Jason mentioned that evening. "Did you notice how ragged their jeans are and how their shoes are falling apart?"

"What are you thinking?" I asked, already guessing the answer.

"Call Nelly's mom and see if we can take the boys shopping."

"And Felipe?"

"Felipe's fine. Toro takes care of his clothes. It's the poor cousins who need help."

Veronica and Daniel's father fished for a living. Their mom, Lidia made tortillas and tamales at a nearby restaurant, along with embroidering cloth napkins and tablecloths. Although their parents worked hard, they had no extra spending money.

"Speaking of Toro, do you want to spend any time with him before you leave? You might like him if you get to know him. I can always invite him over for a glass of wine." I tried to look serious.

"Keep Toro as far away from me as possible. It's bad enough to know he lives next door. I have no desire to see him or talk to him!"

၈

The following day, Jason and I boarded the local bus with three pre-teen boys in tow for a shopping day in nearby San Sebastian.

"Jason wants each of you to pick out a pair of shorts, jeans, a shirt, a pair of shoes, and two t-shirts," I said, after entering the department store.

The boys scattered, looking through racks of clothes in their sizes.

Ten-year-old Jaime brought two pairs of shorts to show us. "Which of these is better, Jason?" he asked, delight in his brown eyes.

Jason helped him choose.

"And what about these jeans?" he asked a few minutes later. Again, Jason helped him with the better choice.

A short time later, the boys were ready for Jason to pay for their purchases. Nearing the checkout counter, Jorge and Daniel, both eleven, stopped to look at deodorant and cologne.

I saw Jason smile. "Go ahead, boys, get what you need," he said.

"Gracias," they both replied.

"What about underwear and socks? Do you have enough?" Jason asked through me.

The boys shrugged their shoulders and shook their heads.

"Go ahead, go get some," he said, giving them all a smile of encouragement.

On the bus a short time later, Jason and I watched three happy youngsters look inside their shopping bags and talk amongst themselves.

"You're a good man, Jason," I said and squeezed his hand. "Now...you want to work on loving our neighbor?"

"No. That's your job," he said, and looked out the window.

⁓

In mid-January, two weeks after Jason left, Jessica brought me an invitation to her mother's baby shower. "She's having a girl, right?" I asked.

"Yes, Rebecca. Mommy's naming her Kelly. Will you come to the party?"

"I will, Lord willing," I answered, reminding myself to shop in San Sebastian for something pink and 'girlie' for the new baby-to-be.

A few days before the baby shower, Cesar stopped by to fix a leak in the upstairs bathroom. "What are you listening to?" he asked as he walked into the house. "At first, I thought you were watching English-language television, but you don't have TV service."

I laughed. "No, no television service. It's a DVD—a Christian sermon on living a positive life."

"I don't understand the difference between Catholic and Christian, Rebecca. Isn't it the same religion?"

"Kinda," I replied. "Catholics and Christians both believe in God, the Holy Spirit and Jesus, the Son of God, but there are differences. For example, Catholics pray to Jesus Christ along with Saints and the Virgin Mary. In the Christian world, we worship and pray to just Jesus or God."

Sitting in chairs by the pool, Cesar and I spent an hour talking about the differences and similarities in our beliefs and found there were more similarities than differences.

"I haven't been to church for some thirty years, Rebecca," he said. "Well, except for weddings and baptisms. I've tried reading the Bible, though. I started at the beginning, in Genesis, but then I got bogged down and confused."

Nodding in understanding, I stepped inside my bedroom and returned with two Spanish Bibles. "Here, start with the New Testament. Actually, start with 1 John. It's about love...that is the basic message of Christianity. Jesus Christ loves you. So love Him by obedience to His word and love your family. Love your neighbors. Do good."

Cesar thanked me for the Bible and flipped through its pages. "Cesar, would you do me a favor?"

"Sure, Rebecca. What?"

"You're friends with Toro, right?"

"Friends in that we say 'whatsup,'" he answered. "It's too dangerous to be his enemy. I stop and have a beer with him now and then. Years ago, we worked together in construction. I keep my distance now."

"Well, here's the thing. I feel God wants me to love Toro in the Christian sense of the word...to love his soul. But he closes down when the word 'God' comes out of my mouth."

"That doesn't surprise me, Rebecca, given his lifestyle. I'm surprised you even try."

"It's this desire I have to reach him, Cesar. Who knows, maybe he will repent and leave the drug world."

"You're kidding, right? You don't just walk away. A guy I know got involved big time with drugs and a gang in the United States. He left that mafia life behind and came back to Mexico. He'd been here for a couple of years, doing well. A new life. Until someone, sent from the States, came into his home in the middle of the night and killed him. One shot. Boom."

I slumped down in my chair. "Dang. I guess I am naïve."

We stayed silent for a moment, each in our own thoughts.

"Even so...are you willing to give Toro a Bible for me?" I asked.

Cesar stared at me, and I smiled.

"*Por favor*? Please? Would you give him this New Testament during one of your beer-drinking-construction-guy moments...?"

"Why don't you give it to him?" he asked.

"Because I don't think he'll take it from me. He'll just shut down. You can tell him I gave it to you, and you're giving it to him as a favor to me."

Cesar half-smiled. "All right. I'll look for the right moment. But Rebecca, I know this guy. He's hard-hearted. He's made people disappear that went against him or pissed him off."

"What does that mean, 'he's made people disappear'?" I asked.

"He's killed them or hired someone to kill them. It's part of the stay-on-top drug life. If others are coming for your plaza, and you know it, you get to them first. You eliminate the competition."

"That's so hard for me to believe, Cesar. I don't want to believe my neighbor is capable of killing someone."

"That's why people tell you to keep your distance, Rebecca. You're braver than most...the way you interact with him."

I grimaced. "I don't know if it's brave...or stupid. I'm just moving forward on faith."

❧

Nelly's baby shower was an excuse for another party— although mostly women attended this one.

I looked around at chairs filled with beautiful young women in their twenties, already with three or more children. Nelly introduced them as her childhood friends. Most had become mothers before the age of sixteen.

"How did you meet your husband?" I asked Sarah, a gorgeous dark-eyed girl who was sitting at my table.

"We met in middle school," Sarah answered. "Later, we dated and '*él me robó.*'"

"I've heard that expression a lot," I said. "It means he 'stole' you?"

"*Sí*, that's how we say it. We went out, we spent the night together, and he knew I couldn't return home to my parents...so, '*él me robó.*'"

"It that still the way it is?" I asked. "Does pre-marital sex still mean you are 'married' to your boyfriend?"

"That depends on the parents," Nelly said, sitting down in the chair next to me. "And it may be different in cities. In rural areas with more traditional families, parents believe if you think you're old enough to have sex, you're old enough to start your own life."

"That's very different from how we treat the subject up in the States," I told the young women at the table. "Although I don't promote pre-marital sex, I'd personally never force my daughters to be forever tied to their boyfriend because of a sexual encounter. But then, I come from a different culture and must respect your parent's traditional values."

I came upon Toro leaving his house a few minutes later. "Hola, Toro," I said, greeting him as he rounded a table filled high with presents. "Are you heading out to hide from all these women?"

"Nope. I'm staying here."

"Really?"

"Ricky, Miguel, and I will sit over there," he said pointing to the place on the curb where I often sat and talked with him, "and watch you women play your silly games."

"You three don't have better things to do?" I asked. "Like sell beer or something?"

"Nope."

"Well, what silly games does Nelly have planned for us?" I asked, smiling.

"It's not Nelly. Lupita and her mom planned this. From what I heard, it's first food and then the games."

After a scrumptious lunch of shrimp tacos, salad, rice, and beans, the guest participation began. I attempted to meld into the background, holding Jessica on my lap. I entertained myself talking to Jessica while watching Nelly's friends play "pin-the-tail-on-the-baby," followed by the "walk-around-with-a-raw-potato-between-your-legs," game and other equally funny stunts.

Then, after a short break, Lupita called for volunteers for the next sure-to-be-funny event. I hid behind Jessica, using her as my shield.

"Rebecca!" someone yelled.

I looked up and followed the voice to Toro, Miguel, and Ricky. Toro motioned me forward.

I shook my head. "No."

He motioned again.

"You, Rebecca. Papi wants you to play." Jessica giggled as she hopped off my lap and pulled me to the middle of the circle of at least sixty women.

I pulled back.

"Here, Rebecca," Lupita said, laughing. She handed me a miniature baby bottle, a large square piece of white cloth, and a bib.

I looked at the items, feeling foolish. "What's this game all about? What do I do?"

"You run to that line of women standing over by Toro. Choose a partner, bring her back to these chairs, and wrap her in this 'diaper,'" she said, pointing to the large piece of white cloth. "Then put this bib on her, get her onto your lap, and feed her the bottle. The first team to complete all that...wins."

Oh, no! How embarrassing. "Okay."

"Why is Toro involved in this game?" I asked, surprised at his participation in a baby shower.

"Oh, he's not involved. He's just sitting where the women are lining up."

Once the chosen six participants had diapers and bibs in hand, Lupita yelled, "Go!"

I ran the fifty feet as fast as I could, hearing Toro and his brothers cheering me on. I chose my friend Celia as my "baby." Rushing back to the chairs with five-foot-tall Celia in tow, I diapered her on the outside of her shorts, and tied the bib around her neck. I plopped Celia onto my lap and stuck the bottle in her mouth. "Done!" I yelled. "Did we win?"

I looked first at Lupita and then over at Toro, who sat with a big smile on his face. I saw him chuckling and shaking his head, "No."

"No, Rebecca. Sorry," Lupita answered. "But you won fifth place!"

Dang. I thought I was running really fast!

As embarrassing as it was for me to run my out-of-shape body up and down the dirt street in front of so many younger people, the experience gave me the opportunity to bond in a special way with my Barrio community and neighbors. I also felt a bit closer to Toro, showing my willingness to accept him, his family and friends. *Maybe it will make a difference as I move toward reaching him for a higher purpose.*

෬

I visited Nelly at the beer store a few days after the baby shower. "Hey, sweetie. Your baby shower was a lot of fun. A bit different from baby showers I'm used to."

"Thanks for coming, Rebecca. Toro still laughs remembering your efforts to win that game."

"Oh no! How embarrassing!"

"No, it was all in fun. Thank you for taking part."

"Well, I'll need to get into better running shape before your next baby," I said, smiling. "By the way, I'm leaving tomorrow for the States."

"I remember you said you were going up north for a while. For how long?"

"A month. I miss Jason and my kids."

"You have four kids right?" she asked.

"Yes. Sophia, Fernando, Antonia and Summer. They've all been here in La Perlita at one time or another."

"I know I've met them over the years. Antonia used to braid Veronica's hair, right?" Nelly asked.

"Yes, and Teresa's too, when Teresa and her brothers lived here with your parents. My kids love La Perlita, but are too busy with their own families and professions to visit very often."

I paused a moment remembering how full my life and swimming pool used to be with my own children visiting and the five neighbor kids coming over to play.

"I'm also going north because I have a new 'thirty-day agreement' with Jason," I explained. "We don't want to be apart more than thirty days at any one time. He was here in December, we've been apart all January, and now I'm going north for February."

"Wouldn't it be easier if he'd live here with you during the season?" she asked.

"Ya' think?" I said with a laugh. "That would be ideal. I have tried to convince him to stay longer, but he won't. I can't make him love it here like I do."

"Sure would be nice if we could control our men," Nelly said, grinning. "Your daughter, Antonia is pregnant, right?"

"Yep. Part of the plan is to be with her for the birth. This is her first child."

"When is she due?"

"On the sixteenth. And your due date is the twenty-third?"

"*Sí.*"

"Well, you keep baby Kelly inside. I'll go to California to meet my newest grandchild. It's a girl, too, and they're naming her Belen. As soon as she's born, I'll come back for you to have Kelly. How's that sound?"

"What date do you return?"

"March first."

Nelly chuckled and caressed her large stomach. "I don't think I can hold her in that long, Rebecca," she said, her dark eyes smiling.

"Sure you can. Just keep your legs crossed."

We both laughed.

"Where's Toro?"

"Inside, recuperating."

"From what now?"

"The usual, too much drinking and staying up late into the night. He's impossible."

"Has he always drunk like this?" I asked.

"No, not when we were younger. Now I think he drinks to block his feelings." Nelly hesitated a moment. "I'm sure that's what he's doing. But he won't admit that."

"Can I ask you something...personal?"

"Depends," she said.

I looked around to make sure we were alone. "I know what Toro does—besides beer sales," I whispered. "Not that I would tell him I know. I wish he *was* only a beer sales guy."

Nelly appeared to resist where the conversation was heading, but then nodded once, which I took as permission to continue. "I've heard there's no way to get out of the drug world at his level...but can't you guys pack up and go somewhere new?"

Nelly looked like she wanted to cry. "No."

"Nowhere?"

"No," Nelly replied, shaking her head. "As they say, 'once in always in.' It's true."

I wanted to hug her, but felt a wariness come over Nelly. "We don't talk about this, Rebecca. Sorry."

"It's okay. I won't say anything to Toro. I want him to think I don't know about the drugs...that I'm just a naïve gringa. It's better that way."

Nelly shrugged and cleaned the counter in front of her.

After a few moments of silence, I turned to leave. "Well, I need to finish packing," I said, acknowledging the closed subject.

❧

The following morning, I stopped to say goodbye to Toro before Tina took me to the airport. I found him in his hammock.

"Good morning, Toro," I said, sitting down on a nearby chair.

"Hey. You're leaving today?"

"Yep, back to the States."

"For how long this time?" he asked.

"A month. Will you watch my place for me while I'm gone?"

"I always do," he said.

"Thanks. Give me a hug. I'll see you soon."

❧

Soon after, Tina arrived to drive me to the airport. "Who are you planning to visit during your time in the States?" she asked.

"The first two weeks I'll be with Jason. And, since Summer lives nearby, I'll spend time with her and her baby, Alessandro. Then I'll drive to Santa Rosa to visit Antonia and go shopping for the any last minute things she needs for her baby."

Tina laughed. "That works. Will you see your older kids?"

"Yes, Summer, Alessandro, and I fly to Arizona after Belen's birth to see Sophia and Fernando. I want to be in the audience when Sophia receives her bachelor's degree in nursing. Jason will meet us there."

Thinking about all I had jammed into four weeks made me laugh. "Dang, I'm already tired just thinking about that schedule I've placed myself on!"

237

"As usual, you're stuffing a bunch of family activity into a small time frame, sister dear," Tina said. "Tell my nieces and nephew I send my love."

"I will." Opening the car trunk, I added. "I'm hoping to make it back before Nelly has her baby."

"Good luck with that," she said.

❧CHAPTER THIRTY-ONE❦

California

Back in California that evening, I rested my head on the back of the passenger seat in Jason's Murano. I looked out the car window, enjoying the distant Sacramento city lights as we traveled east on Highway 80. "I've talked to Felipe about his education," I said.

"What about his education?"

"You know how much he loves my place. He wanted to know how I got such a big, beautiful home. I explained my years of education, which led to my well-paying profession, and over time, extra money to build the house."

Pausing for a moment, I thought back to my conversation with Felipe. "He said he wants a house like mine. I told him if he stays in school and chooses a good profession, I'll sell him my place for a steal of a deal when he's thirty."

Jason laughed, turning down the car heater. "That won't happen," he said in his usual matter-of-fact tone. He shook his head in amusement. "A more likely scenario is that he'll take over his father's drug business, have more money than you and I combined by age thirty, and buy all the houses on your block."

"I like my version better," I answered, and changed the touchy subject. "Speaking of the kids, Veronica, Daniel, Felipe, and Jessica all say hello. I'm supposed to give you a hug for them."

"I'll make sure you do, then," he teased with a big smile. "So, how's your friendship with Toro?"

"It's progressing. We sit on the curb facing our houses...and talk."

"What do you have in common to talk to him about? Crime? Sales numbers? How many people he's killed?"

"Jason! Stop that. He's a real person inside that scary gruff nature. This week we talked about construction costs. My neighbor Gloria wants to add a second story on her place. And we talk about disciplining techniques with Felipe, which by the way don't seem to work for long," I said shaking my head.

"What techniques?" Jason asked.

"I worked with Nelly to set up an easy behavior modification program. Every time he changes out of his school uniform without his parents asking, and completes his homework, he gets a star. When he goes a whole week with daily stars, he gets ten pesos."

"How much is that—a dollar?"

"Yes. He then saves those pesos for something he wants...like a new soccer ball."

"And? How is it working?"

I laughed. "He hasn't made it through a whole week yet...but we're early in the game. I really want to find out what makes him tick so I can help Nelly motivate him. He's going to be ten."

"What do you expect from him? He's impacted daily by both his father and uncles' actions. He sees and lives their dysfunction and has no role model for success, Rebecca."

"It doesn't mean he can't choose a different life," I interjected. "I want to believe in something positive. But I'll admit it will be tough with his resistance to school. Lack of education sets a kid up for fewer life choices."

೧CHAPTER THIRTY-TWO೧

February 11, 2013 Eleven days later~ Toro~ La Perlita

Panicked, Toro grabbed his phone. With shaking hands he called his brother, Julio. "It's happening, Bro," he said. "They're coming for me."

"Who?"

"*Assassins*, working for the Knights Templar cartel. They have arrived in the area and are here to take over all the plazas up and down the coast. Including mine."

"*Los Templarios*? How do you know?"

"I got a call. A hitman murdered my contact up near Vallarta early this morning—he was assassinated in his bed."

Toro steadied his voice. "The guy on the phone told me to leave or they'll kill me."

Toro heard Julio take a deep breath and let it out. "Did you verify that info about your contact?"

"I did. I talked to his brother. It's true."

"Are you leaving?"

"No. I'm going to fight. This is my town."

"Toro, think about this. How can you go up against Los Templarios?"

"I've had armed bodyguards ready for months...just in case. I've called them. They're ready to go. I'll station them at both entrances to my street...four up in the sports field, and another four right inside the tree cover by Rebecca's house."

"*Maldita sea, carnal.* Damn, Bro. This sucks."

"It does suck, Julio. I'd heard rumors the Templarios hooked up with the Sinaloa Federation to finish off all traces of La Familia. But that was over a year-and-a-half ago. Damn. I should have taken it more seriously."

Toro started pacing, phone to his ear. "I figured we were too far out of the loop to be a target. The guy in Vallarta says there are criminal groups operating in Michoacán and Jalisco. Splinter cells commanded by former members and leaders of La Familia *and* the Knights Templar cartels. They're vying for power and territory. It's a train wreck headed this way."

"I'm on my way, Bro. I'll have Miguel meet me there."

Ten minutes later, Miguel and Julio's vehicles careened down the dusty street to Toro's house.

Toro met them outside. He gulped down a bottle of Tecate and reached for another as his brothers arrived.

"Does Nelly know?" Julio asked, slamming the door of his truck.

"No. I don't want to scare her. She's nine months pregnant, man!"

"Where is she?" Julio asked.

"At the clinic for her weekly checkup."

"Anybody else here?" asked Miguel, sitting on the edge of the chair he placed next to Toro's.

"We're alone. Chuche and Ricky are out making deliveries, and Felipe and Jessica are in school."

Julio grabbed a bottle of beer from the cold twelve-pack at Toro's feet. "Does this have to do with the police officer who was killed yesterday? The news says the four guys who killed him are cartel members. They took off in a black SUV and headed toward Autlan."

Dread filled Toro's chest. "I'm sure it's connected. I need to keep Nelly and the kids safe."

"What about Sandy and Marco?" Julio asked.

"I don't think they're at risk. I'm the target, and I'm here."

"Is Rebecca next door?"

"No, she went up to the states for a few weeks."

Julio started pacing. "Why don't we all go to the big house? We have an arsenal there. Isn't that why you've been buying guns and building that place...as a safe house?"

"The high walls are up, but it can still be penetrated in several spots. It's just not ready. It's in an isolated area to launch a counter attack...but it's not ready."

Taking a deep breath and squaring his shoulders, Toro said, "I'm not going down without a fight."

Miguel stood up. Fury sparked in his eyes. "We can't let them come in here and take over, Bro. Let's call Esteben and talk about this."

"No. Esteben wanted out of this life and I agreed. I'm not going to bring him back in now."

Already on edge, Toro jumped as his phone rang and vibrated in his pocket. Taking it out, he looked at the caller ID and then answered. "Whatsup, Alvaro?"

"Toro, those crazy *sicarios* just took out Alfonso and his whole family in Villa Caliente."

Toro felt his heart pounding into his chest. He slammed down the phone. "Damn!"

"Toro, what happened? You look like you've seen a ghost," Miguel said.

"It's Alfonso! I've known the dude since we were fourteen!"

"What about Alfonso?" Julio and Miguel asked.

"Dead. He and his whole family. He refused to give in to the Templarios."

Toro swore, filling the air with the anger he felt in his soul. "I will fight those suckers. For Alfonso. For his family. For La Perlita. For my family."

"You better think about how you're going to fight them, Toro. These guys are psycho. Cold-blooded killers. Hyped on meth and coke. You know that. Get Nelly and the kids and go!" Miguel begged his big brother.

Toro took a long swig of his beer and crashed the bottle against the wall. "No!"

Toro spent an hour that evening talking with his guards at the entrance to the sports field. "I knew this might happen, just not so soon," he said, keeping his voice steady. "Expect guys in black SUVs or on motorcycles. Probably with Michoacán plates. They'll be guys you don't recognize."

Eight somber men dressed in black, with an array of sport caps on their heads, nodded.

"Don't be afraid to fire if you see them heading my way. You guys got this?" he asked.

"*Sí*," answered Pedro, a tall muscular man in his early thirties. The others nodded, following Pedro's lead.

"Why haven't you notified your guys on the police force?" Pedro asked, after lighting a cigarette.

"My guys are out of a job. They were among the ten policemen the new county police chief fired last month—they didn't pass some damn test they were given. But you'll be well paid for this."

"All right, Toro. We got you," said Alfredo, a tall, lanky fellow wearing a Chivas sports cap.

"Good. Starting now, seven o'clock. Break up into two shifts, twelve hours each. You're protecting this one long block—from here to the row of trees at the end of the block. Between your two stations, you'll have good visuals."

Toro exhaled, attempting to calm his pounding heart. "Make sure no cars or people come onto this street unless you know them."

∽

After a sleepless night, Toro awoke and gathered Nelly into his arms. He pulled her close and placed his hands over her belly, wanting to savor the moment. His baby girl kicked against his large hands. "She's active this morning," he said gently.

"She's kicking like she wants out of there," Nelly said, and caressed his hands. "What's going on with you, Toro?" she asked. "You tossed and turned all night. And I felt you get up and walk outside several times. Is something wrong?"

"Just business stuff, Nelly. Nothing for you to worry about."

෨

After a late breakfast, Toro drove up to the top of the street and pulled into the sports field. "So far, we're okay," he told Pedro, who'd come on shift at 7 am. "Did your guys see anything last night?"

"Nothing suspicious. They say it was quiet all night."

"I just got off the phone with a friend in San Sebastian. There's fighting—right now," Toro said. "That's what, some forty minutes away?"

"Yep," Pedro replied. "I heard that, too. It's the police and Federales. They're heavily armed. They're after those guys who killed the police officer Monday. They apparently shot several gang members in a safe house on the outskirts of San Sebastian."

"Well, let's keep our fingers crossed. The threat may end right there," Toro said.

Leaving the guards, Toro drove the ten blocks to Sandy's house to spend a few minutes with her and Marco.

"I love you, Marco," he said, holding back emotions as he buried his face in his son's neck.

"Why are you so emotional?" Sandy asked, brushing fingers through her hair.

"Things are happening I need to deal with," he responded. After hesitating for a moment, Toro continued, "Sandy, if anything happens...I want you and Nelly to raise the kids together. You got that? No more of this fighting between the two of you."

"Come on, what are you talking about, Toro. What's going on?"

"Do you promise to do that? Become friends, good friends, for the kid's sake?"

"Yes, Toro."

He saw the panic in her eyes but didn't explain.

"Okay. We'll bury our hatchets. But why?"

Toro dared not speak. He kissed Sandy and Marco one more time and drove away, not looking back.

I can't believe this is real. How can this be happening? And to think I used to feel indestructible.

Driving past the guards on the corner, willing their presence to comfort him somewhat, he returned home to find Nelly waiting for him outside.

"Something wrong?" he asked, concerned.

"Felipe's teacher called. The principal wants to see us in her office at one o'clock."

I don't have time for this! "What now? Toro asked, frustrated.

"I guess we'll see at one," Nelly responded.

At precisely one o'clock, Toro and Nelly entered the school office. They found Felipe sitting in a corner, head down, messing with the laces on his sneakers.

"Thank you for coming," the principal said, motioning Felipe forward.

Toro, Nelly, and Felipe settled into the chairs placed in front of the principal's desk, waiting for her to speak.

"We're now past the mid-term, and Felipe is a month behind his classmates," Miss Estela said, looking at the notes in front of her. She removed her glasses and laid them on her desk. "He has to catch up or he'll lose this whole year."

Toro nodded. "Any suggestions?"

"Discipline at home, teaching him respect for authority, and positive role-modeling, for a start," she said.

"Anything else?" Toro asked, looking into the principal's eyes, reading her frustration with his son.

"Maestro Julio mentioned a friend of yours, a Señora Rebecca. She helped Felipe stay on track last year. Is she still around? Otherwise, his fourth grade teacher, Maestra Gina, will work with him after school. He needs to catch up."

"We haven't asked Rebecca to help with homework," Nelly said. "She's working with the Mayor on social projects in town, and more important, we want Felipe to be responsible. He's..."

Toro interrupted. "Thank you for your time. Felipe, Nelly, let's go." *I can't just sit here and act like nothing is happening. I'm about to jump out of my skin! And what if they come for me here and take out Nelly and Felipe, too?*

Miss Estela sighed and closed the file in front of her.

Nelly turned to Toro, a puzzled look on her face, took Felipe's hand, and followed without saying another word.

"What was that about, Toro?" she asked as they got into the car. "You agreed to come and then you just cut the meeting short and order us to leave. What's going on with you?"

"I don't have time, right this minute, Nelly. Have Maestra Gina start working with him." Toro kept his hands on the wheel, looking side-to-side, making sure no unknown vehicle approached during the short drive home. "What's for lunch?" he asked to change the subject.

"Barbecued chicken and rice," Nelly replied.

Toro parked his white Ford F-250 in front of the house and walked around to the passenger side to help Nelly maneuver her very pregnant body out of the seat. "I don't know how I'll last another two weeks," she said, holding onto Toro's arm and waddling into the house.

"Thanks for bringing Jessica home from school," Nelly said as her sister-in-law walked out of the kitchen to greet them.

"No problem. Why don't you rest while I finish lunch?" Lucia offered.

"That would be great. Felipe, go change out of your school clothes and start your homework."

Felipe obeyed without a word.

"Can I help you, Tia?" Jessica asked. "I'll set the table."

"Sure, sweetie," Lucia said, patting Jessica on the head.

Nelly gazed out the living room window at Toro, who was lying in the hammock, staring at his phone. *This is so strange. He says he doesn't have time to sit in a school meeting and now he just lies in his hammock. And, by now, Felipe would have been cussed at, kicked in the rear, and grounded to his room...I wonder what Toro is waiting for?*

❦

An hour later, with the family together at the table for lunch, Nelly watched Toro pick at his food. "Are you okay," she asked concerned.

He hesitated and then nodded.

Felipe looked at his mom and then his dad. He stayed quiet...also picking at his food.

"It's my birthday in two days, you know," Jessica chattered. "I'm excited about my party on Saturday. All of my friends are coming. Did you buy my presents, Mommy? I'm going to be a princess. Right? It's going to be so much fun..."

Standing, Toro captured Jessica's face in his large hands and kissed both cheeks before walking outside.

"Mommy, is my daddy okay?" Jessica asked. "He didn't eat anything. And why didn't Felipe get in trouble today?"

Lucia raised her eyebrows at Nelly as if asking the same thing.

"'cuse me," Felipe said, and went to his room.

Nelly looked at Lucia and shook her head. "Something's going on...I wish I knew what."

❦

At five o'clock, after two agonizing hours of hoping the inevitable would not arrive, Toro's phone rang. The screen read, "Blocked number."

"Yeah?"

"Tell your guards to leave," the voice said.

"What guards?"

"The ones in the field at the head of your street and the ones in the tree cover at the other end. You think we're stupid?"

Toro hesitated.

"Tell them to back down *now*. Or they're dead, you're dead, and your family is dead."

"What..." Toro stopped talking, realizing the caller had hung up. Panic threatened to suffocate him. *Fight them? Give in? Risk the lives of friends and my family? How many are there? Can we defeat them?*

Leaving his hammock, Toro stepped into his truck and started the engine. He dialed his phone. "Pedro, call your guys off."

"Why, what happened? I told you we got you."

"Just call them off and leave while you can."

"You sure you want to play it this way?" Pedro asked, his voice escalating.

"It's me they want. I don't want your deaths on my hands, too."

"Oh, man...you sure?"

"I'm sure. I'm leaving an envelope here with Nelly with your pay."

"*Bien*, dude...if that's how you want to do this. What are you going to do?"

"I expect the *cabron* will call back and tell me."

Sitting alone in his truck, cold despair hit Toro. A brew of pain, sadness, disbelief, and mind-numbing fear swirled through him. The reality of approaching death stared him in the face.

At six-fifteen the second call came in. "Leave your house, drive around the block, and head into the Barrio," the voice said.

"And if I don't?" Toro asked, trying out one last moment of defiance.

"We'll delight in killing your family first and then you."

Leaving the truck running, Toro hesitated, took a deep breath and walked into the house. He looked at Jessica playing with her Barbie dolls on her bed and tears formed. *So innocent. So full of life.* He brushed a tear away and kissed her on the forehead.

"I love you, Papi," Jessica said. "Are you going to work?"

"Yes, sweetie."

Felipe cringed as his father approached. Toro sat beside him on the couch and gathered him into his arms until he felt Felipe relax. "You be good," he told his son.

Finally, he went into his room and found Nelly napping on their bed. He lay down next to her and cuddled for a second, knowing he couldn't risk waiting too long before obeying the order.

Nelly awoke. "Toro?"

"Nelly, I need to leave. You take good care of the kids. Remind them often how much I love them." Losing the battle to hold back the tears ready to overcome him, he bent down, kissed her stomach and turned away.

"Toro? Toro, you're scaring me!"

Without another word, Toro left his house, stepped up into his truck, and drove away.

↬CHAPTER THIRTY-THREE↫

Same day, California

Shortly before my daughter, Antonia's due date, I drove the two hours from Sacramento to Santa Rosa. A friend of the family had gotten me a hotel suite where she worked, just five minutes from Antonia's house and two minutes from Kaiser Hospital.

Sitting in the living room of my luxurious accommodations that afternoon, my laptop "dinged," announcing a new Facebook message. I clicked on the screen and glanced at the laptop clock—six-fifteen Mexico time, making it four-fifteen California time.

"*Hola*, Rebecca," the text read.

"*Hola*, Cesar," I responded.

"How's life in California?" he asked.

"Good. Just here hanging out with my daughter, waiting for the baby to make an entrance."

Cesar and I shared several texts about a cleaning project I wanted completed before my return.

"What's going on down there?" I finally asked. "I heard from a friend that there's a gun battle in San Sebastian."

"That was yesterday," Cesar replied. "A police officer was killed by some cartel members. They got away, but the police later found a safe house. There was a shoot-out. The police took out several Templarios. At least that's the rumor around town."

"*Templarios*? The new cartel up in Michoacán? Is La Perlita okay? We're in the height of the tourist season. This isn't good."

"We're okay here, Rebecca. Don't worry."

I asked his opinion on the impact of Los Templarios trying to get a drug hold in the coastal area, when Cesar said, "Hold on, Rebecca. Something's happening!"

"What?"

"I don't know...gun shots or loud firecrackers. Sounds like it's coming from the sports field. Let me check. My wife and kids are there. I'll get back to you."

Less than five minutes later, Cesar texted: "Those were gunshots, Rebecca. It's Toro."

"Toro what? What happened?"

"*Se cayó.*"

The phrase literally meant "fallen." What did Cesar mean? My mind reeled with the possibilities as I dove into denial. *Toro has 'fallen'? Is he hurt? Or is it Toro is 'down'? Is he dead?*

"Cesar, I don't understand..."

"I have to go, Rebecca. Stuff is happening. I'll contact you later."

His messages stopped.

I stared at a blank screen. Confusion and fear overwhelmed me.

"Sis, did you hear gunshots just now?" I asked Tina on the phone moments later, panic setting in.

"Gunshots where?" Tina asked.

"In or near the sports field by my house?"

"No, but then I wouldn't...it's too far away. There were gunshots in San Sebastian yesterday..."

"No, Sis...this was just now."

"Sorry. I don't know. Call your neighbor, Gloria."

My hands shook as I dialed. "Gloria, what's happening down there?"

"Nothing. Why?"

"I'm hearing reports of gunfire."

"I don't think so, Rebecca. There must be a celebration in the sports field. I heard firecrackers go off," she said. "By the way, did Antonia have her baby?"

"Not yet, we're still waiting. Listen, I have to go. I'll see you soon."

I dialed Antonia. "Honey, something's going on in La Perlita. There was gunfire. Cesar said Toro *'se cayó.'* Do you or Lalo know how I should interpret that word? I'm freaking out here."

"We'll be right over, Mom."

The phone went dead.

Five minutes later, I opened the door to Antonia and her husband, Lalo, a young man originally from the state of Michoacán. "Lalo, what does it mean if Cesar said *Toro se cayó*...what is that slang for, because it literally means he fell."

Antonia and Lalo remained silent for a moment and I saw the sadness in their eyes...and I knew.

"Mom, Toro's been killed. That's what it means."

"No!" Collapsing onto the corner chair, I closed my eyes and cried out to God, *It's too soon! I've failed. I was waiting for the right time to talk to him about You. Forgive me, Lord.*

"Oh, my gosh...the kids, Antonia. They'll be so scared. I need to be there."

"Mom, calm down. They have a big family. They'll be all right for a while. You're going back down in two weeks. They'll be okay."

Cradling my face in my hands, I tried to calm my fast-beating heart. *Antonia's right. I have things to do here. She's ready to go into labor at any moment and Summer and her baby are coming down for the birth...and I want to see Sophia graduate from nursing school.*

Stay calm. I can do this.

"Lalo, what do you think happened? Who would want to kill Toro? The cartel?" I asked.

"I know little about the Mexican mafias since I moved here to the States, Rebecca, but didn't you say Los Templarios are the splinter group of La Familia?"

I nodded, dreading the obvious.

"La Familia dominated our town in Michoacán. When they decide to take over new drug territory, they mow down anyone in their way. That's why my family left our hometown. So, if Los Templarios are like them, that's probably what has happened."

I shook my head. In reality it really didn't matter who had killed him. He was dead. Sadness overwhelmed me. *Why should I care so much? He was a drug lord, for heaven's sake. But I do care.*

"Nelly's pregnant with Kelly, Antonia. This will devastate her. Oh, geez...." Deep sobs overtook me. *Baby Kelly will never know her father. Jessica's life of bright skies, Barbies, and the papi she loved so much...forever changed. Poor Felipe...how will he cope? Is somebody there for him?*

Antonia caressed my shoulder. "Mom, it's okay. She has a mother and sisters and people around her."

"I know. And I'll be okay, honey. I will. This is so hard to believe. I just saw him. And hugged him. And asked him to watch over my house while I'm gone."

Antonia and Lalo left after they were certain I was okay.

Curling up on the hotel bed, I cried—and prayed—for Toro's soul, and for his family.

⁂

Cesar was offline all evening and my mind raced through possibilities, including the possibility that the news was wrong. I wanted to believe the news was wrong. *Maybe Toro was shot and fell down and he's not dead. Maybe there are lots of people dead. Where did this happen? In the sports field? That's so close to home. Who was with him? Are his brothers alive? Were Nelly and the kids with him?*

After a fitful night, dreaming of Toro's lifeless body and his children crying, I awoke early and fortified myself with prayer and coffee. *I gotta know for sure what happened!*

Opening my laptop, I found an email from Tina. "Good morning, Sis. Good news. There's no gang left here in La Perlita. They were shot in San Sebastian. Those who weren't killed were transported directly to a jail in Guadalajara. The news says the police were in full gear as were the gang members. It was a big shootout. Time wise, I think the Federales shot Toro to clean up La Perlita before the big shootout in San Sebastian."

The Federales shot Toro? Really? Toro was shot...but is he dead?

I closed out Tina's email and opened one from Christine, an American friend living in La Perlita full time. I longed for news. Anything to keep my grief at bay. "Rebecca, we just read that the police had a shootout last evening in the north part of San Sebastian. Two narco-traficantes were killed, and seven arrested. The police confiscated four AK-47s and lots of other arms and ammunition. On the police side, there were state police, municipal police, and one other organization that I couldn't figure out, but I think is probably the federal anti-narcotics team. The county administrator has requested and received five trucks of state police to stay in the county indefinitely. The army is also out in force, patrolling. I read that the navy is helping, too."

Another email popped into my Inbox from Tina. "Sis, I found out it was the drug people who killed Toro, not the Federales—the same gang that shot up San Sebastian. Everything is back to normal now; we are feeling safe again."

Toro is dead. I have to acknowledge that. But how can Tina say things are back to normal? They'll never be back to normal for me.

"Hey, Tina," I responded. "From what I'm hearing that *is* what happened. Toro was killed by rival cartel members. I don't know about La Perlita being 'safe,' though, as you say. Whoever took out Toro has now taken over his plaza—and who knows who that is. I expect they came to take over the entire San Sebastian area drug trade. Looks like the police have a lot on their hands. I think La Perlita was better off with Toro in charge. At least with Toro, people knew who the 'bad guy' was."

᷈

Cesar came online an hour later. "Sorry, Rebecca. So much happened last night, and then I ran out of minutes on my phone and I couldn't get back to you."

"That's okay. I'm getting basic news in from others. What did you see? And what was Toro doing in the sports field?"

"He wasn't in the sports field. The machine-gun round just sounded as if it happened there."

"Machine gun?"

"Yeah. He was gunned down with an AK-47."

"OMG, Cesar. Let me call you."

Cesar answered moments later.

"Okay, tell me what happened," I said. "We can't text fast enough for me to get it all."

"From what we're piecing together, he left his house in his truck, drove around your place, and headed down further into the Barrio. He was just two blocks from my house."

"Was he alone?" I asked. I felt fear and sadness filling me.

"Yes."

I wiped away the tears running down my cheeks. "How did they get him Cesar?"

"People nearby say it looked like he was headed toward the house he's building. He was driving fast. Two guys on motorcycles cut him off at a corner. He stepped on the gas to get away but they shot out the right side tires."

"I can't believe this, Cesar. I feel...numb."

"Unfortunately, the life of a drug lord is a short life, Rebecca. Witnesses say the truck flipped onto its side. Then a black pickup with tinted windows pulled up and a guy in the back of the truck fired through the passenger window. Toro never had a chance to defend himself."

Hanging up the phone, I let the tears fall unhindered.

Once I had my emotions under control, I called Jason. "Hi, honey."

"Hi. Well...do we have a baby girl?"

"No, not yet. Antonia's not even in labor. She's had sporadic contractions but nothing steady."

"How are you doing? You sound sad. What's wrong?"

"Toro's dead." I fought back the tears threatening to overtake me again.

"Dead? When? How?"

"Last evening, assassins from The Knights Templar, the rival cartel I told you about...they killed him...with an AK-47. He didn't have a chance."

"What about the kids? Are they safe? Was Nelly with him?"

"They're safe. They were all at the house. The hit men attacked while he was driving alone out in the Barrio...on the other side of the sports field. Cesar just filled me in on the details."

Jason hesitated a few moments. "I'm sorry for you, Rebecca. I know you cared about him. But honestly? He was a scumbag, so I can't come up with any remorse, sympathy, or empathy for the guy. However, I do feel bad for Nelly and the kids. Are you heading back down?"

"I thought about it. But my priority right this moment is Antonia and then Sophia's graduation. I'll go back as planned on the first."

I exhaled pent-up emotion. "I feel like I failed Toro, Jason."

Tears interrupted my words.

"You failed Toro? That's crazy, Rebecca. You were nicer to him than any sane person should be. You risked your own safety to be close to him—to attend his parties, to care about his children, and to pursue that friendship of yours with him."

"But I wanted to lead him to Christ. I'd given Cesar a Bible in Spanish to give him. I wanted to *save* him."

"Save *him*? You felt responsible for saving Toro's soul? Toro didn't want to be saved. I think it's very unrealistic that you could 'save' him. Plus that's not your job. Get over it!"

"Why are you so harsh when it comes to Toro, Jason? Why do you think only good people deserve to be saved?" My sadness turned to anger. "He deserved salvation. Everybody does!"

"Honey, calm down. I'm not against helping the unfortunate or reaching the lost...but Toro was evil."

"It's not who 'we' are, Jason. It's who God is. God wants to help the lost."

"If God wanted him helped or saved, Rebecca, He would have made it happen."

I let out another deep breath, confused about what I believed concerning Toro and his salvation, about how things should be and what I'd wanted to happen. The night before, when I couldn't sleep, I imagined Toro crying out to God, asking for mercy as he saw the bad guys rushing at him.

My Pollyanna personality always wanted the perfect fairy-tale ending.

"Are you still there?" Jason asked.

"Yes."

"Having said all of that, Rebecca, I respect your heroic efforts to do what you felt in your heart regarding Toro."

"God told me to love my neighbor..."

"You did! Don't you get that, 'Miss Mother Teresa'?"

I rebelled against Jason's teasing. "I'm not trying to be Mother Teresa! But I do want to obey God."

"You loved Toro, Rebecca, even though he didn't deserve your love. You overcame your fear—remember how scared of him you were in the beginning? You conquered fear and reached out to him. And you loved Nelly, Felipe, and Jessica—and even liked Toro's loser brothers. You love all of your neighbors and so many others there in La Perlita. When are you going to take off the backpack-of-guilt for not *saving* him and accept that you did good. That you'll always do good...because that's who you are. And that's what I love about you...even though you drive me crazy with your risk-taking!"

"I know, but..." I stammered.

"But what?"

"I waited too long. I was waiting until Toro was ready to hear. I started to talk to him about God one day...and he shut me down and walked away...so I waited. When somebody isn't ready to hear, it's like throwing seed on hard ground."

Jason laughed. "There you go with your biblical metaphors I never quite understand. So, tell me what you would have said to Toro when you felt his ground was soft, or ready, or whatever."

I half-smiled at Jason's attempts to amuse me. Then I sat up straight in the chair and took a deep breath, letting it out slowly. I visualized Toro sitting by me on the curb where we'd sat together so many times. I saw myself touching him on the knee, for just a moment, praying silently for the right words.

"I'd say...'Toro, Jesus died for us sinners. He loves you and me, no matter what we've done. And just like you love Felipe with all his rebellion and disobedience, God loves you...no matter what. We can't change our past, but God can and wants to. All you have to do is acknowledge Jesus as God's answer to our sins and ask for forgiveness. He'll make you new again through His grace and mercy.'"

I wiped tears off my cheeks. "That's what I wanted to say, Jason, when the time was right, when the ground was ready to accept the seed of truth."

"Well, then...?"

"He died too soon." Tears fell.

"Who knows, Rebecca? Maybe Toro reached out to God as he saw the danger headed his way. That's not for us to know."

❧CHAPTER THIRTY-FOUR❦

March 1, 2013

Two weeks later, I boarded my Alaska Airlines flight from Sacramento to the state of Jalisco, Mexico. Looking out the airplane window, I thought back with contentment at the wonderful moments I'd shared with my family. I reminisced about the long hours at the hospital holding my daughter's hand through a difficult labor, as she and Lalo waited to welcome a very late baby Belen into the world. I smiled at the memory of sitting next to Jason and my son, Fernando, in the Arizona nursing school's auditorium watching my firstborn, Sophia, graduate with honors. *One proud momma.*

I already missed my family, but knew I'd see them again in one month's time.

"Ladies and gentlemen, we have started our descent and preparation for landing. Please make sure your seat backs and tray tables are in their full upright position. Make sure your seat belt is securely fastened and all carry-on luggage is stowed underneath the seat in front of you or in the overhead bins…"

The announcement pulled me out of my memory mapping and into "we-are-here mode."

I'll finally get to hug Felipe and Jessica.

Tina waited for me outside the baggage area, finishing her cigarette. "Not as much luggage this time," she said, burying her cigarette butt in a nearby ashtray.

"No time for shopping this trip," I said and hugged my sister close.

"I'm so sorry about Toro, Rebecca. You must be devastated."

"I am."

"Have you heard from Nelly?"

"Yes. We exchanged texts a few days after Toro's death. She told me about the viewing on the thirteenth and burial on the fourteenth. I let her know I was praying for her and the kids. Then, a couple of days ago, I told her I was on my way. She said she delivered Kelly by cesarean on her doctor's advice— because of her delicate emotional state. Kelly is a week old today."

"Oh, wow. So what will happen? How will she live without Toro? How will she support the kids?" Tina asked as we got into the car for the drive to La Perlita.

"Good questions. I guess I'll find out. I'm sure he left money somewhere, and I know he has several properties she can sell."

I opened the car window to feel the warm air on my skin. "Cesar told me only a handful of people attended Toro's wake," I said. "That's sad, since hundreds always attended his parties."

"Why so few?"

"I suspect for the same reason Cesar didn't attend. Fear that the cold-hearted hit men would return and kill everybody at the wake."

"I don't think that would have happened," Tina said. "There's truckloads of Mexican military here, driving up and down streets in the Barrio and through downtown. There are navy ships out in the ocean and police stationed on street corners."

"Wow. Isn't that a bit of overkill? All this because of Toro's death? How important was he?"

"From what Joaquin explained, it's more about making sure there aren't any residual cartel members left who may want to take over this area. There are gun battles waging between the military and the Knights Templar cartel throughout Jalisco, pushing them back into Michoacán."

I shook my head in disbelief. *Wow.*

"Are you glad Toro is gone?" Tina asked.

"No," I replied. "A few years ago, when he first moved in next door, I wanted him gone. But I got used to him if that makes sense." I thought back to my silly antics with Toro, things I'd attempted to make him laugh—like pushing his hammock to wake him up, or the night I drank right out of his cup and choked on the tequila. The memories made me smile.

"I think I actually came to depend on and love my neighbor, Tina. And now, I feel vulnerable."

"Vulnerable? How so?"

"Over the last few years, I've come to see Toro as my protector. As the locals would say, 'You never have to worry about anybody breaking into your house or doing you harm, Rebecca. You have Toro.'"

Tina glanced at me. "It was true, Sis. Even Joaquin said that. So now what?"

"I've been thinking about that since he died. It's time I return to reality and put my faith back in God...not in a man."

We sat in silence for a few minutes as sadness again engulfed me.

"Do you have more details about what happened that day?" Tina asked.

"Some. I talked to Daniel, Nelly's twelve-year-old brother, on the phone a week after the killing. I called to talk to his mother Lidia, but she was at work."

"What did he say?"

"He was playing outside his house with two friends when he heard what his friends said were firecrackers. Daniel thought it was gunfire. He grabbed his bike and went to the restaurant where his mom works. She was there with his older brother, Ruben. They both thought they'd heard firecrackers, but Ruben went with him to find out."

"We have so many firecrackers going off around town, it's no wonder everybody thought firecrackers," Tina said.

"That's true. But, as Daniel and Ruben got near, they saw throngs of people running to a spot about a block from the east edge of the sports field. Ruben looked over the heads of the crowd, saw a white truck on its side, and knew it was Toro. But Daniel says he didn't recognize the truck. It wasn't until he saw Esteben, Julio, Miguel, Ricky, and Chuche screaming and pushing through the crowd that he knew."

"Oh my gosh. How sad, Sis. How sad."

We sat in silence as the miles sped by, both lost in our own thoughts.

"Do you know how Nelly found out?" Tina finally asked.

"Yes. Daniel and Ruben rode back to the restaurant to tell their mom, but as they approached she came rushing out with a startled look on her face—saying someone told her Nelly had fainted. She didn't know why. Daniel told her about Toro and they took off running to the house."

"And the kids?"

"Somehow, Felipe already knew. He ran to Daniel as they neared the house, crying—saying, 'somebody killed my daddy.' When Daniel went inside to check on Jessica, she was still unaware, playing with her dolls on the bed."

I exhaled deeply and wiped a tear from my cheek. The vision, through Daniel's eyes, of what happened that day still overwhelmed me. I gazed out the car window as we approached the turnoff for the Barrio.

"Are you okay?" Tina asked.

"I will be. I can't even explain why his death has affected me so much, Sis. It's amazing my level of emotions and grief...I set out to love him, as precarious as it felt at times, and I guess I really did come to love him."

"I think you really cared about him...but you've always been that way, little sister. You were always the one in our family to champion the cause of the less fortunate."

"I worry about Nelly and the kids." I stopped talking and stared out the window.

Tina broke the silence. "By the way, how was Antonia's labor?" she asked.

"Long. Antonia was two weeks late and then the hard labor lasted over twelve hours," I replied, glad to change the subject. "I'd been with Antonia all day and night, but had to leave early that morning to catch the flight to Arizona. Belen arrived twenty minutes after I left the hospital room." *I couldn't save Toro and I missed my granddaughter's birth.*

"Oh, no! You wanted to be there."

I chuckled. "Yes, I did...and I was...for most of it. But what we'll remember are the last twenty minutes I wasn't there."

Moments later, Tina pulled up in front of my house. I opened the passenger side door and Felipe came running. "Oh, sweetie," I said, stepping out of the car and holding back tears. I bent down to hold him close.

"My daddy's dead, Rebecca," he said, sadness etched into his young face.

"I'm so sorry."

After thanking Tina for the ride and letting Felipe help with my luggage, I said, "Let's go see your mom. Is she okay?"

"No. She cries a lot. But I have a new baby sister."

"I heard. I want to meet her."

Felipe led me into his house. Toro's mother, Maria smiled from the kitchen as I entered. The aroma of simmering chicken filled the room.

Embracing Maria's small frame, I said, "I am so sorry for your loss, Señora Maria."

"Gracias, Rebecca."

"How long will you be here?" I asked, not surprised to see Nelly had family support with her.

"My husband and I came for Toro's wake and the novena. I'm staying on for Nelly's forty days of confinement. Then we'll see."

The Catholic tradition in Mexico is to hold a wake for twenty-four hours once the mortuary delivers the body to the family's home. After those twenty-four hours, there is a burial ceremony at the local cemetery with songs, tears, and impromptu prayers for the deceased.

I knew from my texts with Cesar and Nelly that they buried Toro on Jessica's birthday. Instead of celebrating her seventh birthday that day, she stood at her mother's side as they buried her beloved father.

The day after the wake and burial, a novena begins at the family home. For nine days, family and friends visit to show support by uniting to pray the rosary.

"I'm glad you're here, Señora Maria. I've been worried about Nelly and the kids."

"*Gracias*. But between Lidia, Lupita, Veronica, and me...she's had plenty of care," she said kindly.

"Wonderful."

Felipe took my hand and led me into his mother's bedroom. Jessica looked up from the middle of the queen-size bed, where she lay touching her baby sister's cheek. "Rebecca!" she squealed and crawled off the bed to hug me.

Sitting down on the bed, I pulled Jessica close and kissed her forehead. "*Hola, mi amor.*"

"My daddy's an angel, Rebecca. He went to heaven, but now he comes and looks in the window and he protects us," she said, with her sweet smile. She spoke quickly while hugging me tight.

I kissed her forehead again, allowing her hug to warm my hurting heart. "You're right, sweetie. He'll always be your angel. He loved you so, so much."

I looked over Jessica's shoulder and smiled at Nelly, who was watching us from a rocking chair in the corner of the dark room. "Hola, Nelly. I'm so sorry."

She nodded, tears glistening.

Felipe approached and handed me some pictures.

"What are these?" I asked, flipping through them. "Oh, geez...."

"The bad guys shot my daddy," Felipe said, pointing out several gunshots in his father's forehead.

I gazed at a picture of Toro's still body, lying in a coffin in a white button-up shirt. Tears gathered and ran down my cheeks. *How sad for Felipe to walk around with pictures of his father in a coffin.*

Baby Kelly whimpered and Nelly struggled to get out of the rocking chair. Setting Jessica aside, I rushed the few feet to help her stand. We embraced.

"I'm so sorry, Nelly. How can I help?"

"We're good, Rebecca...for now." Nelly started to walk toward her newborn baby daughter, but stopped a moment, retrieved a piece of paper from the dresser top, and handed it to me.

"What's this?" I asked, scanning the official-looking document.

Nelly sat down on her bed and gathered Kelly close, cuddling her. "That arrived today. It's the title for the lot in front of your house."

I glanced at the document, noting the words "land title" on the top and looked back at Nelly, not understanding.

"Toro purchased your park before he died. I didn't know he'd done that until this arrived today," she said with a sad smile.

Speechless, I shook my head in disbelief. I thought back to my conversation with Toro a year earlier—telling him I hoped the owner would not find a buyer for the lot, so the kids would always have a place to play.

"He knew how much you cared about that piece of property, Rebecca. And how much work you put into it," Nelly said.

Felipe and Jessica looked up at me, smiles on their faces. "Did you two know?" I asked.

They both shook their heads.

I smiled, thinking of Toro contacting the owner of the park and purchasing it—without saying a word.

"I think he wanted to surprise you, Rebecca," Felipe said.

Thank you, Toro. May God's mercy cover your sins and bring you close to Him. I will never forget you. I promise to be here for Nelly and your children—loving my neighbors.

❧

275

A week later, I heard laughter and stepped out onto my balcony. Felipe, Jessica, Veronica, Daniel and Marco played in the park across the street. Veronica pushed Jessica in the tire swing and the boys chased after their soccer ball.

You're still here, Toro. Good and bad you'll always be here. Rest in peace my friend.

❧EPILOGUE❦

2016

The house next door and the park are now empty. Children's laughter and their frequent visits are no longer.

Following Toro's death, military soldiers raided Miguel's home and found an arsenal of weapons and ammunition which they confiscated. The authorities allowed him to go free if he refrained from all involvement with drug dealing, instructions he reportedly followed. He married and moved to Michoacán.

Nelly disappeared in April, 2015. Witnesses saw her talking to two men in a dark SUV moments before her disappearance. Her family is devastated. Esteben contacted me the day following Nelly's disappearance, asking me to return for the kids and take them to the United States. Although my heart wanted to, and Jason encouraged it, I knew I had no authority to take custody of the children.

Toro's assassination brought Esteben out of "retirement" and at age twenty-six, right after the Mexican military pushed the Knights Templar cartel out of Jalisco, he and Julio took over their beloved brother's drug plaza. Their angst and anger over Toro's death changed them. They became power driven—extorting money from the family businesses in La Perlita and condoning home robberies. They routinely brandished arms and threatened residents.

A new cartel took over the Pacific Coast area and in August 2015, Esteben and Julio "disappeared." They are believed to be dead.

Following Nelly's disappearance, the San Sebastian Social Service Department awarded custody of the three children to her mother, Lidia, and her older sister, Lupita with summer vacations awarded to Toro's parents. The kids were with their paternal grandparents in Michoacán at the time of Esteben and Julio's disappearance. They never returned to La Perlita.

Veronica's dream was to work in the hospitality industry. In August 2015, based on her excellent grades and exemplary behavior, she received a full scholarship through a local scholarship program, allowing her to attend a vocational high school.

In early April 2016, three masked men, wearing baseball caps and wielding knives, forced their way into the family home when Veronica's father opened the door to go to work. Veronica escaped over the back wall as the assault began and ran for help.

The assailants tied up and stabbed her parents, her brother Daniel, and her cousin Jorge. The adults and Jorge recovered from their injuries after several surgeries. Fourteen-year-old Daniel, stabbed in the upper spine, was left unable to walk and remains confined to a wheelchair.

The perpetrators escaped and there have been no arrests to date. Following the assault, news reports stated the "investigation extended into the state of Michoacán." Some believe remnants of Toro's family in Michoacán instigated the assault; blaming Nelly's family for complaining to the new cartel about Esteben and Julio's aggressions against the town residents. Nelly's family denies any involvement in their disappearance. Her parents and siblings are in hiding.

There is no overt drug cartel activity in La Perlita. I have heard there is an organized crime group managing the drug trade in the state of Jalisco, but their presence is unseen in the village. The locals are happy to report, "*todo tranquilo*"...all is calm now, and I have reclaimed my paradise, although it is bittersweet.

Before Nelly's disappearance, I purchased the park land from her and landscaped it. It sits waiting for the next generation of children to move into the neighborhood.

I still winter in La Perlita, missing my sister who recently died. La Perlita just isn't the same without her. I continue to love my visits with Chato and Marta, and my on-going conversations with Tony on our drives in and out of town. I still work with the town leaders to make La Perlita a better place.

This small fishing village off the Pacific Coast of Mexico, remains my little piece of paradise.

ᚼREADERS GUIDEᚼ

Questions and Topics For Discussion

Part One~

1) At age 13 and with no resources, Toro decides to stay behind in La Perlita when his family moves back to Michoacán. Have you, or anyone you know, ever confronted this major adult life choice at such a young age? Or, given the circumstances, would you have made this choice? Discuss.

2) As a young teen, Toro exhibits an entrepreneurial spirit when he starts his own panga tour business. Do you think that spirit contributed to his decision to go into the drug business at age16?

3) Toro, as a young man, sent a large portion of his weekly paycheck to his family to pay for his brothers' school expenses. Have you or anyone you know ever made that level of sacrifice for your siblings? Explain.

4) If Toro's father had not been an angry, alcoholic, abusive husband would Toro have made the life choices he did?

5) Do you think it was inevitable that Toro "became his father?" Why or why not?

6) Had Nelly's parents forbidden her to leave their home, do you think she would have obeyed them or followed Toro, anyway? Can you think of pivotal instances in your life that forever changed the trajectory of your life?

7) While in Michoacán with his family, Toro made the decision to participate in managing marijuana crops and then the decision to return to La Perlita and sell drugs. Had he not returned to La Perlita how do you think his life would have ended?

Part Two~

8) If you were Rebecca what would you have done to resolve/cope with the conflict presented by the neighbor? Have you had a similar conflict and how did you choose to resolve it?

9) Friends and family counseled Rebecca to stay away from Toro. What would you have counseled her?

10) Which of Rebecca's actions do you think made Toro willing to include her into the perimeter of his life?

11) How would you describe Toro's and Rebecca's relationship? And why?

12) Do you think Toro should have (or could have) escaped his demise by leaving La Perlita and the cartel behind?

13) Jason was verbally and vehemently opposed to Toro as a person for his life choices. Did you find yourself agreeing with him or with Rebecca when it came to Toro? Why?

14) How do you think Jessica and Felipe's early life experiences will impact their adulthood? Why?

15) Which crossroad in Toro's life most affected the outcome of his life? Why?

16) Which parental decision most affected the outcome of Toro's life?

17) Given this story, who do you think bears the most responsibility for the drug war in Mexico? The Americans who purchase the drugs and sell arms to the cartels; or the cartels for growing and exporting the drugs into the United States? Why?

18) Did Toro's decision to choose his family's life over his own surprise you? Why or why not?

19) Did you find any "good" in Toro, like Rebecca chose to do? Or, do you think he deserved his ending?

✆ABOUT THE AUTHOR❧

Originally from Redwood Valley, California, Linda (Cassells) Bello-Ruiz, co-founded and directed The House of Hope in San Jose, Costa Rica, a safe-haven for street girls and underage prostitutes. After returning to the United States, she earned a master's degree in Psychology from Sonoma State University in Rohnert Park, California.

For twenty-six years, she worked as a bilingual vocational rehabilitation counselor in Santa Rosa, California and consulted as a vocational expert on disability in litigation for five of those years. The mother of four grown children, she is now retired, dividing her time between California, and the Pacific Coast of Mexico.

Ms. Bello-Ruiz is a spokesperson for a leading organization in California dedicated to increasing awareness of the evils of sex trafficking worldwide, and building restoration homes for rescued victims.

During her months in Mexico, Ms. Bello-Ruiz is active in the town council, spearheads fundraisers, and is the co-founder of a youth scholarship program, providing financial assistance to selected middle school students so they can attend high school.

Ms. Bello-Ruiz's mantra is, "Lord, how can I be of service—what do You have for me today?"

Her award-winning first book, From Tears to Triumph, My Journey to The House of Hope, is available on Amazon.

Contact the author at lmbelloruiz@gmail.com or via her website at www.lindabelloruiz.com

Made in the USA
Middletown, DE
02 August 2022